# COURTING JUSTICE
# IN THE
# GENDER WARS

# COURTING JUSTICE

# IN THE

# GENDER WARS

*A Story of Family, the Supreme Court,
and Gender Equality*

# R.L. SOMMER

TURNER
PUBLISHING COMPANY

Turner Publishing Company
Nashville, Tennessee

www.turnerpublishing.com

Courting Justice

Copyright © 2021 by R.L. Sommer. All rights reserved.

Cover design: M.S. Corley

Library of Congress Cataloging-in-Publication Data TK

9781684424993 Hardcover
9781684425006 Paperback
9781684425013 Ebook

Printed in the United States of America

# TABLE OF CONTENTS

# CONTENTS

# DEDICATION

My grandfather came from Austria to America, worked in a factory in Hoboken, New Jersey, and raised his family as many immigrants did in our country early in the 20th century. When I brought him my first book, based on my Yale Law School doctorate dissertation and published later, he said to me, proudly, "Ronald, work is work. But a book is forever."

As is my debt to him and others . . .

# Introduction

*Courting Justice* is the sequel to *Recusal*, published by Turner in 2020. There, Sydney Emerson and Jacob Lehman met at the US Supreme Court where they worked for one year as clerks to two Justices there. They dealt with issues of law and politics and media at the highest levels in Washington, DC, and while all that was happening, they fell in love. They were an unlikely couple: she a Californian, Stanford graduate, and Rhodes scholar; he a Jersey boy from New York University Law School.

Here, in the sequel to *Recusal*, we follow their lives as they set out as a married couple commuting in California, Sydney as a law professor at Stanford, and Jake as a trial lawyer in a boutique law firm in San Francisco, where they live.

The rest I won't give away here. Read on . . .

# chapter 1

# Fall 2020–Two New Lives

Back from their honeymoon in Hawaii, Sydney Emerson and Jacob Lehman (both kept their birth names, as was increasingly the custom in 2020), entered two new worlds together. Sydney was back at Stanford, fresh from her Supreme Court clerkship, very much at home now as a law professor at her alma mater. Jake was in San Francisco house hunting, about to start his first job in a boutique law firm after clerking. Washington, DC, and the US Supreme Court, their former home and employer, were very far away from their new lives.

🏛

Jake would always remember his first visit to Brock and Arguello for a reason he would not have expected at that time, but one that became clear as he settled into his first job. The San Francisco law firm was in its second generation, having been started by the named, now aging partners who were unlikely colleagues and friends. It was now run by their sons.

Alejandro Arguello was a brilliant and precocious young teenager from a small village in Mexico. He had come to California in the mid-20th century because his father saw a future for him that he knew he could never attain in the small, provincial town his poor family lived in. He was an exceptional student and athlete, a charmer admired in his community where he was viewed as someone who could have a career beyond what was available to him there. His parents and siblings spoke no English, but seeing special possibilities for Alejandro, they were able to find a Catholic elementary school where he would learn the language, if haltingly. His family and friends collected a modest kitty to enable him to come to a new world in California and make them proud by being successful in ways they could not advance nor even imagine.

Young Alejandro Arguello arrived in Los Angeles after a day and night ride by bus. In a classified section of a newspaper he picked up from a bench in the bus station, he found a modestly paying job as a groundskeeper at the University of Southern California's flashy baseball field. In return for perfunctory chores, he also was able to find a simple, free, sparsely-furnished room in a house near campus from which he could walk to work. He worked assiduously, soon added other campus jobs to supplement his modest income as a groundskeeper, and lived a confined life around USC.

Austin Brock was a star pitcher on the USC baseball team. He had an athletic scholarship, though his family was wealthy and he didn't need one. He was a popular man on campus. Austin had trim athletic looks, a magnetic personality, and a wide circle of talented friends who would later become community leaders. Brock met Arguello when he was working near the team practice field. Austin needed someone to catch for him after the student players ended practice and left for their classes and other activities. An athlete himself, Alejandro was thrilled to be recruited. His new university friends renamed him Alex.

An unlikely friendship evolved. Brock was a rising collegiate star whom the Oakland Athletics optioned in his junior year. His family would not let him quit college before graduating, so he took the offered money and stayed at USC, a rising personality on campus, mentioned as a future star in national sports magazines.

His friendship with Alex grew as they worked together on the baseball field. Alex had been a good baseball player in his own right but had no time for activities that did not add to his income. His work with Austin brought them together on a more personal level.

The two young men became friends despite coming from totally different social and economic universes. Alex was ambitious, and he began taking courses at USC in his few non-working hours under a scholarship program offered to underprivileged employees in the union Alex had to join to retain his university job. Austin invited Alex to his family home on occasions. Eventually, the Brock family adopted Alex, seeing his promising future and impressed by his work habits, and his unique friendship with their popular son.

Austin suffered an arm injury at the Oakland Athletics' summer league before his senior year at college. It was a time before medical advances had offered Tommy John surgery to solve his problem. He graduated and married a beautiful classmate from a prominent San Francisco family. Reluctantly, he gave up the idea of a professional baseball career, went to law school, and later "loaned" his pal Alex some of his bonus money to enable him to accelerate his course work at night classes. Eventually, Alex would enter the USC law school on an affirmative action scholarship. Austin had already completed his final year when Alex arrived for his first, where he would excel. His was an only-in-America story.

While Austin worked in a high-visibility, politically-connected job as an Assistant US Attorney in San Francisco, he kept in long-distance contact with Alex. Alex met and married his wife Sophie, who was from a middle-class Hispanic family of overachievers in San Rafael, north of San Francisco, while they were in law school. Austin was the best man at their simple wedding. A few friends from school, one mentoring law professor, and some of Sophie's family and friends came. Alex's parents were his only other guests. He had sent them tickets to travel, and they arrived by bus into what was for them another world, bringing a basket of food for the event, about which the better dressed attendees smiled and whispered.

Alex was ready to seek his first job, having graduated second in his class, behind his wife, who worked for a Hispanic rights organization in Marin County. Austin suggested that he and Alex start their own law firm. It was prophetic, and theirs became the first multi-cultural firm in socially stolid San Francisco. Austin would provide the social status, right club memberships, and political and client connections. Alex operated the behind-the-scenes doing quality research and administrative work and became the perfect avenue into the growing and influential Hispanic and Latino population in the state. Sophie steered interesting cases his way.

In his new life, Alex became a well-known and popular

local lawyer, first among his cultural community contacts and eventually as an equal among Austin's clients as well. The firm prospered. Years later, Austin ran for and won the US Senate seat from California, while Alex grew with their firm into an influential member of the bar, his church, and ethnic organizations—first in California, and later, nationwide.

When Jake arrived at the modern offices of the then second generation, prestigious, and growing Brock and Arguello to start its practice focusing on Supreme Court cases, Austin Sr. still worked in the Senate, while Alex, and later his son, managed their law firm whenever Austin was away (he was rarely home). The firm name remained Brock and Arguello. The formal portraits of both of the elder founders were displayed in the San Francisco office of their prospering statewide operation (they had opened offices in Los Angeles and Sacramento). Eventually, the nation's capital was added to Brock's political presence as the firm's notoriety and success spread. Arguello's son, Alex Jr. (Stanford, Yale Law School), had eventually followed his father as managing partner, Mr. Inside to Brock's socially active son, Mr. Outside, as they became known.

Sydney was on her way to San Francisco from Palo Alto to tour the city with Jake and find their first apartment as Mr. and Mrs. This was not a business visit for Jake, only a perfunctory greeting, touching base at the law firm, his soon-to-be new home. It was fortuitous that when Austin Jr. walked out of his office to greet Jake, he was with the firm's major client, Peter Duffy, a real estate developer, owner of a network of radio stations in several western states, and an influential national power broker and city senior citizen. Jake was introduced to the distracted client who was on his way out as young Austin ushered in Jake. They chatted informally for a moment in Austin's office when they were introduced.

"Jake, say hello to Peter Duffy, who you will come to know when you start work. Everyone knows Peter," he said with a smile. "Peter, Jake is our new recruit, fresh from clerking for Supreme Court Justice White. He'll be running our new Supreme Court practice, starting next week." It was as perfunctory an introduction as was appropriate at the time. No one imagined their introduction would prove to be a huge influence on Jake's career.

After Peter left, Austin and Jake sat in the young Austin's office, where he told Jake more about Peter. He was a self-made billionaire, whose construction and real estate developer business grew, prospered, and led him to other ventures, including owning multiple western state radio stations. He had become a major political and social force in San Francisco, and eventually nationally. He knew everyone, seemed to be at the center of everything economic, social, and political. Peter's broadcast company had been managed by his son and represented by one of the firm's partners, Vincent Fuller, for many years.

Peter had been in Austin's office to discuss a delicate matter involving his son, Pete Jr. ("We're families of juniors," Peter joked when they first met), his business heir apparent. Young Pete, a charming if notorious young man about town, was involved in an embarrassing divorce litigation which was out of the firm's and Vince's area of expertise. Their very public marital split was already in all the gossip columns. Peter was worried that Kelly, his daughter-in-law, had an aggressive lawyer who was out-maneuvering Vince, who Peter Jr. liked but whose father worried wasn't the best at sensitive divorce litigation, which the firm mostly avoided.

Jake asked about the status of the case. Austin explained that Pete Jr. was having an affair with a fading but still beautiful Hollywood actress, and they had been taped on one of their trysts in Mexico.

The conversation then moved to Jake starting work the following Monday after he and Sydney found a place to live, and details of what his introduction to the firm would entail at that time.

As Jake drove off to house hunt with Sydney, he thought about Pete Jr.'s case. Apparently, the lovers had been compromised when, on one of their secret Mexican rendezvous, his wife's lawyer's investigator had managed to put sophisticated taping devices in a pen and a wall plug in their hotel room. Their intimate exploits were in danger of filling the scandal sheet magazines, which would reveal titillating "dialogue" amidst their groaning expressions of passion as they rutted repeatedly every time they were in the room. The family was desperate to keep the proffered tapes out of the public record.

Jake recalled working on a case for Justice White that involved a federal statute which superseded state laws when it came to the use of sophisticated clandestine taping devices in situations where one party agreed to it, but the other did not. That was an anti-trust case Jake remembered more for its facts than the law. The taper had paid a bartender to place an olive with a taping device in the plastic toothpick in one party's martini while he was discussing his New York case with his partners over a firm dinner. Under New York law, the surreptitious recording could be permitted if one party authorized it. California law required both parties to agree to any taping. If the taping was interstate, a federal law prohibited any non-consensual taping, even if it was approved in the state of the taping (in this case, Mexico).

When Jake had a free hour after apartment hunting with Sydney, he drafted a memo from Austin to Peter, laying out why his son's affair could not be exposed on the basis of these tapes, whatever the rest of the evidence might be. The applicable federal statute on interstate investigations saved the day for Peter Jr.—if not his marriage—and it minimized the potential scandal for the Duffy family. Needless to say, Austin was ecstatic when he read it and sent Jake's memo in his own name to Peter. Fuller's motion to dismiss and secure the proffered tapes was quickly granted by the presiding San Francisco trial judge.

When Austin told Jake that he proposed adding his name to the brief, Jake, modest as he was, and a natural interpersonal politician one might also conclude, said his name should not be included. Peter wasn't his client, and Jake wasn't officially a member of the firm yet. Austin never forgot that gracious gesture, but he did let Peter know that the idea had come from Jake.

"I want that young man on our team," Peter replied, and his later mentorship over Jake would color Jake's career.

Alex assured Peter that Jake would soon be part of the firm team, and mentioning that Jake and Sydney were house hunting in a neighborhood where Peter owned a condominium. Peter's company had renovated a light industrial warehouse south of Market Street after the "dot-com" boom brought in high tech companies that transformed the old buildings into a "cool" neighborhood. Peter's personal secretary phoned Alex to tell Jake that there was a perfect apartment for rent in his new luxury condo near the water with a bay view. It was located near an entry to I-280, which would lead Sydney to Palo Alto in about 45 minutes. Jake would be a trolley ride from his office in the financial district near Union Square. The last unrented apartment was waiting to be seen by Jake and Sydney, who were told to ask for the resident concierge, Michael.

Jake's career in San Francisco took off on the best of all fronts.

🏛

Sydney's return to Stanford was like old home week. Lake Lagunita and the foothills surrounding the famous university founded by Leland Stanford in 1885, along with the picturesque quads and arcades on the campus, filled Sydney with nostalgia for the seven years she had spent there. The dean had arranged for her to have a room in faculty guest quarters until she and

Jake were settled wherever they decided. "Why not on the San Francisco side of Palo Alto," he lobbied. He hosted a lunch, attended by many of her new colleagues, to welcome her at the faculty club. Administrative issues were resolved—insurance, class schedules, retirement—"I just got here and you are retiring me," she kidded.

Her course work was arranged to ease her projected commuting: Constitutional law and Supreme Court practice sessions on Tuesday late morning and early afternoon, a new course on gender law Wednesday afternoons, and miscellaneous administrative work on Thursday morning would allow her to live in San Francisco, travel to Palo Alto early Tuesday, and return to San Francisco late Thursday. She could drive between cities and manage a full course schedule. The first-year schedule there also would allow time for her to work on her new book on judicial ethics, which provided a local reintroduction for Sydney.

When they were clerks, Sydney and her DC roommate Ann Horowitz had talked about evolving gender legal matters that had come to legislatures and courts. Each taught a new course on the subject, Ann at University of San Diego Law School. Occasionally they visited each other as guest lecturers to explore this evolving area of law. Years later, Stanford University Press would ask Sydney to propose a book on gender law, and it would become *the* book on this relatively new and evolving subject. Ann would be co-author. In fact, the modern growth of gender issues was a mix of civil rights, domestic relations, employment law, and bits of other fields, like property. Interested women's and civil rights groups called on Sydney to speak and, occasionally, to consult on test cases in a field she eventually dominated.

Between Jake's firm's library, and Lexis provided by the university at her home office, Sydney lived two full, part-time lives, while Jake lived one very full-time life. For both of the newlyweds, life was good.

*chapter 2*

# Words Matter

Jake's chance meetings with Peter at Austin's office, and Peter's helpful outreach in return, eventually would lead to a mentor relationship between the two, and after years, a genuine friendship. Peter would become a surrogate father to Jake, whose family lived far away in New Jersey. They would meet occasionally at the Olympic Club, where Peter often conducted his business lunches. Their friendly lunch habit on Fridays when both were in town became a regular event that they both looked forward to. That connection was cemented when Peter described a situation his broadcasting company was facing.

While Peter was a major real estate developer in California, he also was a major tenant in Washington state, where his growing radio station business was centered. He had started it with a small group of stations in Seattle, and later spread his media holdings into other western states—Colorado, California, and Oregon. Jake's colleague, Vince Fuller, a communications lawyer, handled that broadcasting business for the firm and as a result had reviewed Peter's radio offices' leases as tenant. The original Seattle lease—followed later by others in buildings in Olympia and Spokane, Washington—was causing Peter a major financial problem.

His first lease was a takeover of an existing lease where the tenant decided to move to another neighborhood. Peter's company assumed the remaining two years of that lease at an advantageous rate. The lease also had three additional five-year options "at the tenant's option at a new monthly rate which the landlord could raise to 105 percent of the current rate." The clause was intended to make up for the below standard, low initial rate and later attract good-quality and higher-paying tenants. The landlord then took the position when Peter exercised his option that he could raise the rent on the option period to double the existing rate, plus five percent. That would have converted the original bargain rental to an overly expensive one.

Peter mentioned the matter to Jake over one of their informal Friday lunches at Peter's club.

"Looks like we are screwed," Fuller had advised Peter. He thought about the options that the rent could be raised by 105 percent—no longer the big bargain.

"Wait a minute," Jake responded, after Peter had related the problem. Sliding away his lunch plate, Jake said, "If I remember my fourth grade lessons by my English teacher back in New Jersey, if the landlord intended to raise the rent by double the current rent, plus five percent, the clause should have read '*by* 105 percent', not '*to* 105 percent.' *To* 105 percent would only be five percent over the current lease. The words 'To it' would mean plus five percent of the 'it!' Not a law school lesson I learned, just correct English."

Jake added his modest last remark so as to not sound critical of his colleague Vince.

Peter was stunned, quiet for a moment, and asked, "Is that an opinion, arguably subjective?"

"Possibly," Jake responded, now embarrassed about appearing to be critical of Vince with his spontaneous remarks. "Let me check that I am right."

"How do we do that?" Peter inquired.

"I will run it by Sydney's colleagues at Stanford's literature department." With that, the conversation ended, and they went their separate ways.

Jake asked Sydney that evening if she knew the right faculty expert on language at Stanford who might know if he was definitely right. She did, and when she returned to Stanford the following Tuesday, she took Associate Liberal Arts Dean James Raymond to lunch at the faculty club, showed him the relevant page of Peter's lease, and asked his opinion.

"I absolutely agree that your husband is correct. Sometimes, this is one, a simple word can make a huge difference and lawyers aren't always right in their draftsmanship of documents," Professor Raymond told Sydney.

"Would you answer Jake's inquiry in writing, stating your expert opinion?"

"Why wouldn't I?" he answered. "To me, it is clear and I can run the question by a few others who write about language, to make sure my opinion is solid."

In a week, Sydney received a letter on official Stanford stationary.

# STANFORD UNIVERSITY

Dear Sydney,

I shared your question about the language in the lease your husband is reviewing, particularly whether the option clause language should be "to" or "by" 105 percent. If the intent of the landlord, whose lease was written by him or his attorney, meant he intended to escalate the rental by more than double, he should have written 'by 105 percent,' which would signify he meant by the whole current rent plus five percent. 'To 105 percent' of the current lease would mean the full current rent, plus five percent.

I shared my answer here with three colleagues who specialize in rhetoric and language: Professor Leland Holland at our faculty liberal arts department; my old classmate, now at Yale, Professor Richard Newell; and to assure our conclusion is correct I also contacted University of Chicago Distinguished Scholar of Language Lloyd Greenberg. All three said I might note their assent to my conclusion if it is helpful in resolving the dispute you described to me.

Sincerely,


James Raymond
Associate Dean, Liberal Arts

Sydney brought Jake the letter, and he forwarded it to Peter, advising that "As Vince will confirm, ambiguity in contracts are interpreted against the interest of the author of the words in question, here the landlord. I should think the landlord would not want to litigate the question in court because all his other tenants would be alerted to his attorney's drafting blunder. My guess is that he will settle with you with a non-disclosure clause. Otherwise all his tenants could make the same point and that would *really* cost him, multiplying his lawyer's mistake." As a result, Peter was the beneficiary of 15 more years at the increasingly lower than market rate, a profitable boondoggle.

Needless to say, Peter would never forget this chance conversation (or the considerable money he saved over the next 15 years in his Washington State buildings). As a result, he eventually used Jake on all his work. That included assisting Peter with his interesting, wide-reaching work for the National Democratic Committee, for whom Peter worked pro bono. Jake could charge the DNC on behalf of his firm for his influential new client. He often accompanied Peter when their visits to DC could be coordinated.

Privately, it embarrassed Jake when his colleague Vince later left the firm to teach communications law at San Francisco State Law School.

*chapter 3*

# Living Together in Two Cities

Their joint standard of living now escalated from Jake's barren, tiny bachelor's apartment, and Sydney's shared modest rental in Washington, DC, to what turned out to be the best bargain in San Francisco. Not only did Peter tip off Jake about the one available apartment in the building he owned, but Jake always wondered if he'd given him a special deal on the rental.

When Jake thanked Peter for their good fortune as his tenants, Peter joked, "None of my leases were reviewed by more impressive legal talent than Sydney, and I know you are a careful reader of lease-terms."

Their small but elegant condo was in a slick new neighborhood one streetcar stop from his office, and near both the entrance to I-280, allowing for a scenic, 45-minute drive to Palo Alto, and the San Francisco–Palo Alto train, if Sydney preferred not to drive. It was near the Lowell School, a public school where good students congregated because of its quality teachers. Their new furniture was spare, in modern tastes and style. Their shared large work room could be converted to a guest room when needed, though not often because of their busy and divided lives.

Life was good for them. Friends from Jake's firm and Sydney's faculty colleagues included the young couple in their social world, and Peter and his wife included them in select A-list dinner parties and at the opera and sports events where he held extra tickets for entertaining VIPs. It wasn't long before the *San Francisco Chronicle's* social pages mentioned the attractive young couple, newcomers to town, but surely "comers."

When Sydney suggested that Jake come to Palo Alto for an event of note, he enjoyed the change of scenery and pace and mingling with bright new friends. When they were together in San Francisco, Peter not only opened doors for them, professional for Jake and socially for both, but adopted Jake into his family. Peter's wife, Marie Marino Duffy, a cheerful, open, and attractive aide to all of Peter's life, and Jake shared an immediate attraction to each other, and the foursome became family. Marie was Italian and a great cook, and she and Sydney shared recipes. Peter's chastened son and his new wife were forever in Jake's debt, so he had no jealousy of his father's special feelings for Jake and Sydney.

Act I lasted for about three years. Then Sydney and Jake decided they were ready for a family and their first child, a daughter, was born. Their home-office-slash-guest-room now became baby Maria's, named after her godmother Marie. Stanford provided generous maternity leave, which Sydney combined with her summer months off in academia (when asked why she became a professor, Sydney always replied, "Three reasons: June, July, and August!"). The new threesome had almost a full year together. In San Francisco, they were earning enough to hire a lovely, young, Mexican-American nanny through Sophie's connections, who stayed with them in the baby's room. A few years later, their second pregnancy pushed them to a big house in nearby Diamond Heights, a gracious, capacious, informal home the prosperous and larger Lehman family would live in for decades.

Sydney and Jake agreed about most life and family choices. But they argued about public versus private schools for their children. It was settled, married style; Maria, the excellent student, was sent to Ruth Asawa High School, a prestigious, academically top-notch private school. Why punish her over an academic policy debate? Richard—bright, but not an exceptional student—went to a large public school, which was right for him, it turned out. Both spouses made their points; both children had good experiences.

Life was full. Life was good, very good.

In these years when she was a house mom, Sydney was able to refine and expand her course notes, and begin the gender law book she and Ann would later publish. Her tenth-year sabbatical allowed her to finish the book, and be available to their two children (baby Richard, named after Jake's former boss, Justice White, with whom he had remained in contact, arrived a few years after his sister), and eventually would join Jake occasionally on his trips to Washington, DC.

Jake was away from home often, visiting new clients in other cities, and traveling to Washington, DC, to argue a growing number of cases that increasingly came his way, partly because of Peter, and also because Brock and Arguello was becoming known on the west coast as the go-to firm for its sophisticated national Supreme Court practice. They did find precious family time during those early years, but that time became lessened as Sydney and Jake's work expanded, and their children's lives began to leave the full-time hearth for school, friends, and activities. Life surely moved fast for them.

▥

Their professional lives took off, no surprise, and Sydney and Jake continued to be each other's best allies. Her work at Stanford, and his in San Francisco, developing his high-level law practice, thrived. Their successes in different worlds were complementary, with Sydney as the sounding board for Jake to try out his oral arguments, and Jake editing Sydney's academic writings that propelled her up the ladder of the academic world.

There was one exception, one area where their viewpoints and passions differed. At first, it sparked an unusual debate rather than the usual collegial back and forth of trying out ideas and pressing each other on novel arguments. That first time surprised them both, and would foreshadow a subject that intellectually separated them in different contexts.

It was one of Jake's new cases, a Washington state case he would argue in the early years of his appellate practice. They discussed it over their weekly dinner out together. The case came to Jake on referral from a local Seattle lawyer who represented a religious organization, and he found himself in over his head when the case became a cause célèbre, pitting conservative religious groups against liberal women's groups. Jake was hardly a conservative in religious matters, and he and Sydney agreed on most questions that arose in their everyday conversations and personal practices on that subject.

This case involved a small Christian college professor who

refused to play the "pronoun game of political correctness," as Jake called it when he discussed it with Sydney one evening at dinner when he returned home from Washington after he had accepted the referral. This case was a gender bender.

A transgender student challenged her political philosophy professor—Jake's new client—insisting that the university enforce its rule that students must be referred to in their "preferred gender terms." The professor insisted that the school's demand violated his evangelical Christian beliefs by requiring him to refer to the student, who he perceived as male, as "her," not "him." His student claimed after class that not recognizing her claimed right violated his/her First Amendment promise that there can be no established religion. He/she was belligerent and used profanity when approaching the professor, threatening he'd lose his job if he didn't conform.

The university saw this contentious campus issue as bad publicity when the local press reported on it. University counsel argued that this matter was not a religious one but an academic freedom issue, also predicated on the First Amendment. Language in classrooms, the university claimed, was an academic matter, and it was the professor's obligation to abide by university policies. The professor responded that the university had no business "compelling professors to express ideological beliefs they don't hold and which are as important to university life and campus freedom as student gender rights."

"Colleges are moving toward recognizing an expanded concept of gender held by binary and transgender students," Sydney informed Jake.

"I understand," Jake replied, "and if students get to choose their identity in eccentric ways, they may. But why should professors who see things in a traditional way be forced by their university to speak in a way that they don't believe? What is good for one ought to be good for another."

"Because," Sydney replied, "kids whose gender choices are not traditional suffer and are harassed when they are not identified as they wish to be."

"But my client didn't do that. He's not hostile, couldn't care less about his student's views. He is OK with written IDs being 'Mx,'" Jake added. "He's the one punished by his academic employer for following *his* personal ideas. His student was the hostile one."

"Non-binary students are jeered when they use school bathrooms. Whichever way they declare, they are isolated by the other in those rooms," Sydney advised.

"I never understood gender neutral bathrooms," Jake responded. "I wanted to do lots of new things with girls when I was in college. But sitting in the next stall was never one of them."

Back and forth it went, with a noticeable hint of impatience coloring their informal conversation.

Academic rights advocates split over which claim should prevail. The university took the case away from local lawyers after the administrative stage and retained outside counsel for the appeal to the Washington State Supreme Court and later the US Supreme Court. Jake was brought into this later stage on behalf of the rigid educator by the higher education teachers union. Jake knew the university's outside counsel by her excellent reputation as an appellant advocate but hadn't dealt with her personally.

To both of their surprise, Jake's and Sydney's responses to

his recitation of his new test case differed, and more passionately than usual.

"You never got over that commission you worked on concerning the California Farm Labor Review Peter asked you to chair," Sydney stated, bemused. "What's with you and nouns and pronouns?"

"Yeah," Jake replied quietly, "they wanted to list me on all our stationary and in public media as 'the Chair,' and I told them I wasn't a chair. What was wrong with the traditional chairman, chairwoman, if that was the fact?"

"Seemed old-fashioned of you then, and certainly now when times have changed and individual's gender rights may not conform to their sexual identity assigned at birth," Sydney commented. "Look at your basketball hero Dwyane Wade. He accepted his son's claim to be female."

"Yeah," Jake responded, "biology has been trumped by political correctness, and I don't buy in. Would the Bible now have to refer to Adam and Irv, if Eve decided to change her sex?"

"Since when are you a biblically based originalist scholar?"

It went back and forth after that, and soon the subject was changed.

"When do we need to go tonight?" Jake asked.

"Eleven," Sydney responded, sliding her chair away from the table and lifting her purse to go. Jake noticed her shaking her head as their conversation ended and they walked off.

Two years later, the Washington State Court of Appeals upheld the university's position on the First Amendment. The Union chose not to undertake an expensive appeal to the US Supreme Court, as Jake recommended.

"Told ya," Sydney teased when Jake shared his disappointing news.

"I think we'd have won if we appealed to the Supreme Court," Jake muttered.

"Yeah, maybe with this conservative Supreme Court," Sydney responded.

"The law is what the justices say it is," Jake replied. End of discussion.

*chapter 4*

# Sounding Boards

Sydney and Jake continued their practice from their Supreme Court days of brainstorming issues with each other, even after they moved into different worlds, she in academia and he in law practice. Each genuinely respected the other's mind and found their few debates when they differed helpful, useful. They continued that habit in California, on rides between Palo Alto and San Francisco when Jake occasionally had a reason to join Sydney there, sometimes at their Friday night dinners alone in San Francisco. It was always intellectually thoughtful, even exhilarating, and it added to their personal closeness.

Once, on their drive back to San Francisco from a dinner for faculty spouses Jake had attended, Sydney blurted out as they started their ride home, "Have I got a surprise for you, Jakey!"

"What, you got tenure?"

"No! When Ann was here to work with me this week on our book, she told me she's getting married. To a former student!"

"Who is he?" Jake asked.

"That's the surprise. He's a she!"

"What? Our Ann is gay? And you never guessed?"

"Never a hint. She never had a lover at our apartment. But who, besides us, had time for love in those days?" Sydney teased.

"I saw her with guys we clerked with socially but not romantically."

"I know. It blew my mind when out of the blue, while we were discussing a case for our book dealing with a spouse's right to social security and insurance when their spouse dies, she told me. Like it was an academic issue for our book, not a revelation to a close friend."

"What did she say?"

"Only that they sensed a personal connection but hid it while she was her student. When they met later at some social event it just happened."

"One never knows. Will there be a wedding? Are you the best, what, woman?"

"We never got there, but I bet they are too private about their relationship to have a public wedding."

Once at dinner Jake asked Sydney about a copyright case he was handling representing a performer who was sued by a music producer for stealing a melody from his copyrighted music.

"I don't know about copyright law," Sydney replied. "Only what I learned in the one case we had on the Court dealing with political photography."

"You don't need to know the specific body of law, Syd, I always love to bounce issues off you and invariably get good ideas."

That was the kind of give and take they shared from the start, and for years together in different worlds.

But not so in one subject, they would find. Because Sydney was teaching her gender law course and working with Ann on their book on the subject, they often would talk about Sydney's subjects. In this area, Sydney and Jake often had different perspectives.

Once when Jake mentioned his firm meeting on the subject of maternity leave, their repartee became unfamiliarly contentious.

Jake always said he hated firm meetings though he loved his partners. He couldn't be less interested in firm matters such as which computer contract they should sign, or what pension and retirement policy they should adopt. But when he described a heated debate among partners about one about-to-be partner's request for paid maternity leave, for a longer time than the six weeks' paid leave the firm provided for, Sydney asked what Jake's position was.

"I must say," he answered, "I don't see paying men for paternity leave, nor paying women more than the six weeks that most laws now require, unless there is some medical reason they need more, which would be covered by their general medical and health insurance."

Sydney, unusually for her, jumped at Jake. "Since when is raising a baby a 'medical' problem? And why shouldn't you guys take some time to meet and help with the children you planted?"

"Law firms are economic institutions, Syd," Jake argued. "If men take paid paternity leave, it exacerbates the economic toll on the firm when it acknowledges men too must have that concession."

"Concession, is it?" Sydney shot back. "We better not have

these two children we planned on; we wouldn't want to ask for 'concessions!'" she said sarcastically.

"Why can't it be correct, legally and 'politically,'" Jake responded testily, "for women and men to have different needs and rights? Vive la différence, as the French say." Jake was talking lighter than Sydney appreciated, and she jumped at him.

"We do all the heavy lifting, go through body changes, all the important early childhood care, so we don't consider that some extra time off is 'special' treatment." Her lips pursed, Sydney sat back looking hard at Jake.

Jake didn't relent, and swam into tricky waters. "Women naturally do better at some things—cooking and having babies," he blurted out without carefully choosing his words. "Men lift the heavy packages, usually drive the car even when they are tired, because it is natural." At the use of that word, "natural," Sydney's eyes opened widely, she stared at Jake, and for the first time in all their conversations, sat silently.

Jake recognized that he had hit a nerve, but he didn't understand why this subject would be different from all others when their points of view were respected, even useful, in their opinion making. Their friends and colleagues all noticed that feature of their relationship, and complimented Jake and Sydney.

"You guys sure have the right formula for disagreeing," one of their married friends flattered them, noticing that their opinions in a conversation about mechanical music differed, but their comments had usually seemed to sway each other rather than alienate them.

Jake couldn't resist continuing to plead his case to his obviously annoyed listener.

"Before we got married, if you and I had tried to write a contract for each of us to sign stating who takes out the garbage, gets out of bed to quiet a screaming baby, chase a scampering mouse in the kitchen to see what the strange noise was that might be a burglar, who washes the dishes and who dries, we'd probably never have agreed or gotten married! One of us is better at one thing, even indispensable when it comes to making a baby." At this he tried to lighten the argumentative level they'd reached. "We just naturally step up and assume each other's routine, and it works. I feed the kids when you are away at Stanford teaching, even though you are the better cook. Rest of the time, you do it all with them because when you are there, you *want* to do it. I go to their games on weekends, to give me personal time with them, and to give you a break from that chore, pleasure."

Sydney had no inclination to continue the argument. Things were left at that point, with silence.

Temporarily.

"Remember when there was a pandemic in 2020 and people had to work from home?" Sydney added. "Later, research at Yale showed that women *still* did most of the housework and child care, though both had full time law firm jobs." No response from Jake.

That was the first time, but it wouldn't be the last, that Sydney and Jake clashed over the subject of gender rights. On that one subject, their different genes seemed to separate their intellectual conversation and legal positions.

Sydney's ideas were fueled by who she was and what the differences were between men and women. Jake couldn't understand
why two people who were so close and so thoughtful to each other
on most other divisive issues disagreed on these few subjects.

After another similar spat, Jake brought them to a reasonable
impasse that resolved the itchy moment at the time, and guided
their later conversations about gender matters.

Jake told Sydney about his conversations at the firm, usually
friendly, if provocative ones, about issues that came up. Roger
Williams was an African American lawyer in Jake's firm, smart as
hell, never looking for a fight but always frank about his opinions.
He and Jake would debate the issues of the world, and usually agreed
with each other about topics like staying out of foreign wars, the
fight over balancing the budget, and even in criminal justice matters their differences were few, like regarding the relative blame
for riots between the excesses of police and the over-reactions of
some minority citizens, for example. But the one and only time
they could *not* come to an agreement or even appreciate the other's
point of view, Jake told Sydney, was over affirmative action, an
issue upon which they respectfully but adamantly disagreed. Once,
during one of their unusually heated exchanges on that subject, Jake
had told Roger, "You know what? We are both right!"

"Don't play me, Jake," he shouted, "I don't need to be
indulged by anyone, you included."

"I was shocked he'd think I was doing that. I told him what
I meant, and it may be why you and I disagree on these gender
questions."

"And what is it you told him, that I should learn, too?"
Sydney sarcastically challenged.

"I said, and meant it, that for a black man, affirmative action would, and should, be seen as a way *in* for someone who has been historically shut out. But for others, like we Jews who have historically been kept out of medical and law schools because of quotas, we don't want them! We prefer progress by meritocracy."

"Don't you see?" Jake continued. "Setting a mathematical number on admissions to schools was a way to get black people IN and to keep Jews OUT!"

That seemed to placate Sydney, but not forever.

*chapter 5*

# The Blur of Life

There is a joke about three clergy who are having an epistemological debate about when life begins. As expected, the Catholic priest makes the case that life begins at conception, and he states the Church's rationale for that conclusion. The Methodist minister challenges the priest, making the opposing Protestant argument for why life begins at birth.

"What do you think, Rabbi?" they ask.

"Easy," he replies. "Life begins when the kids go to college, and the dog dies!"

That was the case with Sydney and Jake, after they switched coasts and lives. Each was consumed with their work, Sydney as a traveling academic, and Jake as a conventional trial lawyer with a quite unconventional and sophisticated appellate practice that had him on the road, if not as regularly as Sydney's weekly traipses to and from Palo Alto and San Francisco.

There was a period, years in fact, when time seemed to be a blur. After a few years developing their bachelor, professional, and married routines, along came Maria and a few years later, Richard. Their elegant spare apartment in San Francisco closed in on them with a nanny and children and soon they moved to a large, old Victorian house in a good school district, still amenable to their work lives, particularly Sydney's weekly treks. Their separate lives, several days each week, and their joint one, the other days, were so filled that time seemed to fly by.

Sydney's life in Palo Alto occasionally included Jake when it made sense, and allowed him to include an academic part of his life. Sydney loved the contrast when she came home to San Francisco, the children, and the A-class life Jake had made for them in San Francisco, with much help from his benefactor, Peter.

Jake's tenure at the firm was rapid. He made partner in four years, half the ordinary time at the big San Francisco firms. And not long after that, he was promoted to the firm's management team.

Sydney and Jake carried into their new lives their lifestyles from their Supreme Court clerkships days—obsessive, time-consuming work and intensive personal lives when there was time. When Sydney was home in San Francisco, she made more time for their children, always feeling guilty for the times she was away and could not. Sydney wanted her kids to have what she never had from her mother, and she never quite felt she had time to do that the right way. She and Maria enjoyed those few occasions when they could go to Palo Alto together on some amenable excuse. Jake and Richard developed a mutual passion for fishing, and enjoyed occasional father-son days at the yacht club Jake joined in Sausalito, more for access to the boat he kept there than the club social life for which they rarely had time.

Their home in San Francisco was popular, with the children by day, and Sydney and Jake's entertainment in evenings when they could arrange it. They had quiet, private lives when they were apart, and social ones when they were together in Palo Alto and San Francisco. It seemed they knew everybody, were well liked, and invited by all the "right" people to the "right" events.

As they prospered, they bought a getaway vineyard property in nearby Napa, to which all four escaped when they could. That lasted about five years, when the kids rejected the appeal of open space without their friends and preferred extra-curricular activities. When they sold that property, they doubled their money, which assuaged their personal misfortune.

It seemed they looked up one day and they were 45, established, fortunate, if a bit breathless from the process.

As life drifted into regularity, Sydney and Jake loved their lives together and apart. Their big house in San Francisco was always full of children, children's friends, Jake's family when they could travel (less as they aged), and occasional friends passing through.

Sydney and Jake kept occasional contact with "their Justices," as they referred to their original bosses at the Court. Not so much their clerk colleagues with whom they were intensely involved that year they were together. Except for Ann, Sydney's former roommate, now teaching in nearby San Diego and working with Sydney on her book on gender law. They visited each other occasionally and became a close threesome, eventually four.

Once when Ann stayed with Sydney and Jake at their big house, after a winey dinner and the kids had gone off to bed, they reminisced about the old days. Ann had talked occasionally with their clerk mates, Sydney and Jake less so. All of them held good jobs—a few on faculties teaching like Ann and Sydney; one in the Solicitor General's office, the job Jake almost took and might have if Ann had stayed in Washington; others in big law firms making salaries that their academic and government friends envied.

"Where did we go wrong, Ann?" Sydney kidded.

"You got the best of both worlds, Sydney," Ann countered. "You have the self-indulgent academic life while Jake is providing the grand budget."

"True," Jake responded. "But I work a twelve-month year, and you two work nine."

Ann and Sydney toasted Jake: "We'll drink to that."

⬛

Maritza, their nanny, became a crucial part of the family, the missing link that connected all at-home activities. At one of their Passover seders, an infrequent religious holiday they enjoyed, always with guests, Maritza's influence became clear. When Jake hid the traditional matzoh, and the young attendees went in search of it as is customary, young (then four years old) Maria found it and came running to the table with her prize.

"You know what we call this?" Jake asked.

"Yes," Maria answered, "it's a tortilla!" to rollicking laughter around the table.

Their friendship with the Duffys grew to be full and very personal. Marie recruited Sydney for the Northern California chapter of the ACLU, which became Sydney's way to be active in the city's public affairs when she was in San Francisco. Jake was befriended by many of the Stanford University Law faculty on his occasional visits, and even lectured once a year at Sydney's Supreme Court practice seminar. Jake travelled often, irregularly, as Sydney did regularly, and Maritza relieved that potential problem. The children loved Maritza, and didn't notice when Sydney and Jake were away. Sydney worked at modeling their lives with the children to assure it was the opposite of what hers had been. When they could, Jake's family came to stay at the house with Maritza and the children, and made it possible for them to travel alone together when they had a tempting reason. Family connection was never disrupted.

Jake's family had a house in Belmar, on the New Jersey shore, that they had summered in forever. Each summer, Jake and Sydney and their children spent a nostalgic week there; the kids swam in the ocean and ate ice cream walking on the boardwalk, where Cohen's Cones had lured children and families since Jake was a kid. The elder Cohen, Manny, had died, but his son, known as Ace, had worked at the family's simple wooden boardwalk stand as a teenager and eventually took over the family business replacing Manny. Lines of devotees—families having quality time with young children, self-conscious teenagers clustered with each other—snaked around the block in summer and it was speculated Ace banked a small seasonal fortune, earned cone by delicious (and overpriced) cone.

Sydney loved the family scene, they all did, but especially her because this was a chapter she had missed in her family life growing up.

As the children (and grandparents) got older, those Jersey

jaunts became fewer. Maria and Richard went to west coast summer camps that featured their special interests, horseback riding for Maria and tennis for Richard. Jake and Sydney managed, when their schedules permitted, a week in Hawaii without files and law books, at their honeymoon hideaway. They were the Duffys' guests at their vineyard in Sonoma for weekends, often with others, sometimes just the four of them.

Jake's firm grew in size and reputation after he arrived and their clientele became national, partly because of Peter Duffy's devotion to the firm and his expanding activities, many of which involved Jake. As a result of his predicted successful work, Jake quickly became a star of the San Francisco bar.

Jake and Peter, and Marie and Sydney, became more than business associates, but close friends, almost family. Sydney and Jake had no family on Sydney's side, and on Jake's it was a long-distance relationship—real but distant. Peter and Marie hosted Sydney and Jake more than their young protégés possibly could reciprocate, try as they did. When Peter had his 65th birthday, Marie hosted a lavish party at their club. She asked Peter's special guests to offer toasts when she stood to clink her glass and capture the attention of their 30 dearest and closest friends.

Jake, the youngest and nearest to the select group, was last, but his words brought tears to many of the watching eyes. When he finished, Peter and Marie both embraced Jake, and then Sydney. They told Jake they would keep his words that night in their family memorabilia box.

"I am the newest to have the privilege of joining the Peter and Marie special friends group, but Sydney and I are no less in enthusiasm and the love of our hosts than you all who had a head start in that friendship. Sydney and I came to San Francisco knowing no one. Sydney knew some people from Stanford, but I'm a Jersey boy whose only contact with San Francisco was when our treasonous New York Giants came here. By chance, Peter and I met when I arrived for my first day at Brock and Arguello. But from that moment, Peter and I blended, and soon Marie and Sydney did as well. Peter and Marie became our closest family; we even named our daughter Maria after Marie. Our son is named after Justice White whose hiring me led to my meeting and later marrying Sydney—you can't compete with that Peter—but it was close."

"Next one," Peter interrupted, to laughter.

"People say lawyers talk too much, probably because they are paid by the hour. I won't delay this party longer, nor charge my hourly rates, except to say: Peter, Marie, thanks for letting us into your lives, and embellishing ours. We love you both."

The family had its share of life's problems, none tragic or beyond correction. Richard was a bright boy but inexplicably had bad grades in school, unlike his sister who was a scholastic star. Jake's mother fortuitously discovered the cause on one of her visits, while reading with Richard. She pointed to the manuscript for *Recusal*, the one that Sydney and Jake were writing together, on their table. "Are you proud of what your mom and dad have written?" she asked Richard.

"Why are they *wrecking* us all?" he asked, puzzled.

She realized that Richard's eyes were processing the word "Recusal" in his brain which read to him as "Wreck us all," silent W, so it came out *Rec-us-all*.

As Richard learned after starting school, he was dyslexic. As is often the case, that problem caused troubles in the lives of exceptionally bright young children who never knew the cause and as a result accepted the role of being poor students. When his grandmother noticed Richard's reading difficulty, she mentioned it to Sydney, whose family optometrist analyzed the cause. He recommended they take Richard to a psychologist who would analyze Richard's problem and prepare a psycho-educational report recommending a suitable course of action.

"Imagine the word 'together,'" Dr. Rosen explained to the family. "You and I would see and process it as 'together,' but Richard would see it as *to-get-her*." Later, tutoring by Ann Harris, the dyslexia specialist recommended by the school, changed Richard's life. Moving him to his sister's private school made a big difference because it had special needs experts.

Reading remained difficult for Richard, but interestingly he became a writer, starting with his high school newspaper, writing about his passion for sports. In fact, in an example of truth being stranger than fiction, Richard helped Sydney and Jake finish editing their manuscripts years later. When their book was published, Richard reminded them by toasting "the authors of this great book, *wreck us all*," to laughter around the room.

Richard was accepted at Stanford's remarkable writing program, saving his parents tuition fees, and making them very proud. And it allowed Sydney some further personal family connection to Stanford.

They had worried that Maria, an excellent student who loved her horses, would become an equestrian, as that is what she always replied when asked about her future. With time, and after reading *To Kill a Mockingbird* in high school, Maria decided that—like her parents—she would try law school.

They became the family Sydney always wanted and which Jake had always had, but more so.

One of the practices Jake's family followed on Friday nights was a traditional dinner, not particularly religious beyond lighting ceremonial candles, but a time the family reserved for just the four of them. The idea appealed to Sydney when Jake told her about it, and they followed his family's practice whenever their travels and the children's social schedules permitted. Maria and Richard both enjoyed listening to Sydney and Jake discuss their interesting cases, and occasionally they had comments about their parents' stories.

Most of the family discussions elicited modest interest by the children in their parents' lives, but earnest commentary by Sydney and Jake on the children's lives. That was the idea for Friday night dinners. This one was different.

One conversation Maria started, and the family engaged in, was a roundtable discussion about an event that week in the high school she and Richard both attended.

"A weird thing happened at school today," Maria said, opening the conversation.

"Tell us about it," Sydney responded.

"Yeah," Richard added, "I heard about it but not really the whole story. A teacher was fired for something that happened with her and one of her students?!"

"What was it?" Jake asked.

Maria explained that a very nice, old (she was 45, an old lady in Maria's eyes) English teacher who all the students liked, Ms. Kluser, misbehaved with one of the senior boys, Donald Cooney, a loner. Ms. Kluser did something that got her fired. Maria heard they had sex.

That got everybody's attention. Maria related the facts she knew. Students all liked Ms. Kluser—she was very kind, popular, interested in the kids she taught, and everyone enjoyed her class on writing. Each week, the students would be given a subject to write about, always something on writing rules to follow. Then, later in the week, the kids would read aloud their written papers and the class would discuss them. Ms. Kluser would then sum up the class's comments and give the class her explanation of the rule of writing they were discussing. They'd do that every week. All of the seniors signed up for her course, so she taught two sections, depending on whose writing samples to enter the class were best, and those not best.

"What's 'not best?'" Richard asked.

"That's not the point."

"What is?"

"Well, what I heard was that a quiet kid in her class was a very good writer, and Ms. Kluser often complimented him, and occasionally gave him extra reading to encourage him."

"That sounds like an excellent teacher," Sydney said.

"Yeah, but they had an affair, I heard," Richard chimed in.

Sydney and Jake jumped on Maria's story, trying to engage their children on lessons about sex in high school—it might provide a family teaching moment. It turned out to be a provocative conversation, one they would all remember. It didn't conclude early because Maria and Richard each had some unusually emotional comments. Dinner and family conversation continued until the table candles had burned down.

Facts about the incident eventually became public. Ms. Kluser's young husband had died early in their marriage while serving in the Marines in the Middle East. They had no children, and she taught at the local high school for about 20 years until she was "old"—45, quiet, and attractive. She took an interest in all her students, occasionally took them to Shakespeare plays, and even had an annual end of school year party for them. She seemed to have no other life.

At one event at her house, a student, Donald Cooney, seemed upset and she asked if he wanted to stay awhile and help her clean up from the party, if he had something troubling on his mind. He did. All the kids noticed that he stayed, but no one thought anything unusual of it.

As they cleaned dishes and cups and the party mess, Ms. Kluser asked Donald if something was bothering him, and he opened up to her—as it would later be reported—about his father's drunkenness and violence toward his mother and harshness to him. His father made fun of Donald's constant reading, lack of any life other than school, and umpiring parental disputes, or trying to.

Donald was a loner at school, but he responded to Ms. Kluser's sensitive and friendly way and her compliments about his writing. He was 18, in his last semester, and Ms. Kluser started helping him apply for a scholarship to a nearby college so he could develop his literary skills. It was charged—never proven, but not definitively denied—that the friendship turned into a romance between the young, about-to-be college student, and his teacher, later harshly referred to as his "seducer."

Apparently, Donald's father reported to the school that his young son, near 19 and big for his age, had a suspicious personal relationship with his attractive English teacher. She was called in by the principal and questioned about Donald, and his father's accusation. At first she made earnest remarks about what a sensitive, talented young man Donald is, and that he was appreciative of her coaching help. They'd meet at her townhouse on weekends so she could tutor Donald and assist in his college application, she mentioned proudly. When school officials questioned whether any improper personal activities occurred between them, Ms. Kluser was stunned, teared up, and walked out of the office, remarking, as she left, "This is the ugly work of Mr. Cooney, I just know. Shameful! I won't even honor his slander with a response."

Donald was called in and questioned. At first, he too stared at his questioners, silent for a few minutes, and finally replied. "She's the kindest, nicest person I know. She helps me. I love her!"

The inquisitor took Ms. Kluser's silence and Donald's emotional response in an institutionally defensive way, and recommended to higher school authorities that Ms. Kluser be fired for "unprofessional and inappropriate behavior with a student." Rather than fight an embarrassing public charge, she accepted an offered compromise, a retirement package, and resigned. She and Donald were seen together later occasionally in public, always prompting critical whispers by local observers. Eventually, both of them left town, and weren't heard from again.

Sydney and Jake saw the unusually keen interest both kids showed, and tried to draw them out. Both Maria and Richard were very passionate in their responses.

"She did nothing wrong, and got fired," Maria said, her eyes filling with tears of earnestness. "She was a great teacher. How could the school do this to her?" she asked. "Is that legal? Dad? Mom?"

"What about Donald?" Richard continued, unusually engaged in the conversation. "What if he did love her? Dad? Mom?"

"Good question," both parents responded, quietly looking at each other. Who should respond?

Sydney did first. "You know, kids, teachers have a responsibility to avoid certain personal contacts with their students, however well-intended their feelings may be. She is older, is in a position of power over her students, and is always the responsible party in situations like this. The student's consent can't truly be a consent—they aren't equals. Remember that male gym teacher we read about who took sexual advantage of his students? Everyone agreed he should be fired."

"But he was a man," Richard jumped in. "Donald wasn't a real child, and Ms. Kluser was nice to him. She never *abused* him!"

"If a male teacher abuses a girl student, why shouldn't a woman teacher equally be seen as "abusing" her male student?" Sydney asked. Sydney was acting like a professor engaging in a Socratic discussion with her students.

"She was seen as predatory in this situation, however nice she seemed to her students," Jake added. "Women typically may be sweet and caring. But their personal actions should be judged critically, as the male gym teacher was."

Neither Maria nor Richard really understood Sydney and Jake's explanation. Maria put herself in Ms. Kluser's position, and felt for her personally, as a victim just for being kind. Richard commiserated with Donald, probably considering privately if he might have liked being "abused" by Ms. Kluser.

Later that night when Sydney and Jake discussed the unusual passion their children displayed at their dinner colloquium, they both agreed it was interesting that Maria took the side of defending the teacher, and Richard defended the student.

"So the gender wars start young," Sydney remarked. "Personal sympathies and empathies seem to begin with gender."

"What else could it be?" Jake responded. "Their views come from their backgrounds. You and I have nuanced differences in our views about men and women, based on our experiences. They aren't accultured yet to understand the nature of hierarchal social roles and responsibilities. They will learn soon enough."

"I'm not sure that is a good resolution," Sydney answered.

As parents, as personal partners, as a professor and as lawyers, Sydney and Jake would learn this kind of debate goes on beyond high school; it goes on forever.

After 15 successful years on the Stanford faculty, Sydney was appointed Dean, a five-year period of meetings, administrative obligations, and fund-raising. Sydney taught only one course during this period—her women's rights course that brought attention to the law school and to Sydney in the legal education community. She declined a second five-year term, preferring to focus on her academic work and allowing her more San Francisco time.

Jake's work at Brock and Arguello became the public advertisement of the firm's practice and growing reputation, in part because specialty law firms had become the fashion nationally. That reputation was heightened by its connection with Peter Duffy, who became more and more Jake's mentor in the San Francisco community, and Washington, DC, public and political affairs.

"Our life has become a blur," Sydney remarked to Jake when their second child applied to college, and the parents finally had time to ponder their successful lives. They recalled the joke about the three clergy, realizing that the rabbi's insight, if not ecclesiastical, was correct.

*chapter 6*

# The Wedding Cake Debate

Their magical wedding notwithstanding, who would have thought wedding cakes would cause Sydney and Jake a problem? They had, from their days clerking at the Supreme Court, debated legal issues with genuine views about their positions and respect for the other's. Never had they showed rancor or anger. They continued to be each other's sounding board in their continuing lives in academia and law practice, enjoying their differences and respecting their critiques.

This one time was different.

As was their habit, they reserved one night when they could break busy routines and share an early and private solo dinner at their favorite neighborhood Greek restaurant, Athena. Sydney had prepared dinner for their kids, and Ginny, their relief babysitter, was there to backstop Maritza on her night off. That usually included Jake finishing what he didn't get done in the office, and Sydney working on tomorrow's lecture or her next article. When Sydney was home, Jake would come home earlier than usual, shower, and get into casual clothes while Sydney prepared the kids' dinner and oversaw Ginny. Then they would walk, holding hands, to their Greek rendezvous, and enjoy an informal "How did your day go?" chat while their hovering hosts brought out an ice bucket containing their favorite retsina white wine, and ordered.

"We have your favorite bronzini tonight," the friendly owner advised, and Sydney and Jake both ordered a Greek salad first and shared the bronzini cooked in salt, then skinned and boned theatrically by their regular waiter, an eccentric, elderly Greek straight out of central casting. Sydney couldn't wait to tell Jake about an exciting call she'd gotten earlier from the Women's Caucus, which she had dealt with often as an advisor. "They asked me to take their New Jersey test case to the Supreme Court," Sydney announced.

"Great, tell me about it," Jake responded as he sipped his drink.

"Remember the Colorado case in 2018?" Sydney asked. "About the baker who wouldn't design a wedding cake for a gay couple who admired his artistically designed cakes?"

"Yes, that was a tricky case," Jake answered. "The baker refused to bake an elaborate wedding cake to celebrate their customer's gay marriage. The baker wouldn't do it because his would-be customers had a design in mind, two men atop the cake holding hands and kissing, instead of the usual man and woman. The baker wouldn't do it to their specs for religious reasons, and the Supreme Court upheld his right to deny them his services. I kinda agreed," Jake concluded.

Sydney interrupted, uncharacteristically annoyed. "You agreed?! You don't agree with public accommodation laws? A public business can refuse to serve a member of the public whose lifestyles the owner is critical of? Give me a break, Jake!" Sydney responded harshly.

"I thought you liked brainstorming ideas," Jake responded. "Get some idea of what arguments you'd hear from your opponents."

"Go ahead," Sydney challenged, not sounding truly curious. "Edify me!"

"Well, if someone comes into a bakery and asks for cookies or a cake on display on the counter, and is refused service because he or she is gay, that would be a clear violation of public accommodation laws." Jake went on: "But, if someone comes in and asks the baker to create something on the customer's mind, to create a work of art, so to speak, a painting or sculpture of two guys or gals kissing, or exchanging rings like your new clients, that is more than asking for a can of tuna fish, and more like asking an engineer to design an electric chair if he or she was opposed to capital punishment. And he shouldn't have to."

Sydney challenged Jake, "What if he refused to make a cake because he didn't like that the customer was wearing a yarmulke, or Muslim head covering?"

"That would be different," Jake answered. "The state refusing an application for a driver's license because the applicant wore a covering on her face has been upheld by the Supreme Court as a legitimate public safety regulation."

Sydney answered, "That was different, more like the Court agreeing that states could outlaw use of peyote by some Native American tribes who used it for 'religious' reasons."

"But you can't take away *all* personal rights when peoples' claims are personal and reasonable, not unconstitutional on their face," Jake answered.

"Since when did you become a libertarian?" Sydney went on, abruptly finishing her glass of wine and reaching for the bottle to refill her glass, not like her habit of deferring to Jake to ceremoniously perform that formality.

"Since I decided that political correctness doesn't trump personal autonomy on a touchy issue."

That ended their collegial exchange, and without more debate Sydney changed the subject.

"Maria is going to have to have braces, Dr. R. says. Better put in a few extra billable hours, kiddo!"

So ended their "romantic" night off. The rest of their evening was filled with old married couple trivia, and they returned earlier than usual. Jake walked Ginny home, and Sydney and Jake went separately to sleep.

"Busy day, tomorrow," Jake said as they slid into their big bed.

"Yeah, me too!"

But that earlier conversation would foreshadow an awkward later chapter in their professional lives.

As scholars do, trial lawyers, especially those who specialize in appellate practice, often undergo what they call "murder sessions" to prepare for their arguments in court. Colleagues, or friendly experts, gather to listen to a lawyer present a case-to-be, privately and actively. They interrupt, ask likely questions, and put their colleague through an exaggerated intellectual torment aimed to prepare the advocate for the real thing before the court that will hear and decide their case.

Sydney did that at the Stanford Law School moot court room before a collection of friendly scholars, faculty members, and some representatives of the national women's groups who had underwritten the New Jersey case and recruited Sydney to handle the argument. Ann came up to Palo Alto to assist her old friend and colleague. They did another session at Jake's office before its best and brightest appellate team in the firm's library the day before she flew to Washington, DC, with Ann to prepare for the following Monday at the Supreme Court. They stayed at a funky, small inn in the middle of the city where they wouldn't be likely to be seen, and would be able to dine there in peace and privacy.

Jake had offered to come and provide moral support but Sydney, uncharacteristically, preferred he remain home with their kids, and not add to her nervousness during final preparations. They'd talked through the issues enough times, and there had often been an edge to their arguments.

That Monday, Sydney returned to her former workplace with Ann, who sat with her at counsel table for the first time. Several representatives of the women's group supporting the case, and the two young women plaintiffs in the test case, sat behind them. Only a few of the justices remained on the Court from when Sydney worked there, but the politically adept Chief Justice welcomed Sydney with a smile and a "welcome back, professor" as she rose to "please the Court."

Sydney would keep a copy of the transcript of her argument before the Court in her growing memorabilia file. She didn't need a transcript to remember vividly the challenging repartee between her and the justices on the, some would say rabidly conservative, Court. "Good that I'd had my practice sessions," she thought, though she rarely conceded that notion out loud to Jake.

It did not take long for the mood to change from collegial to contentious. Justice Albert Friendly from Montana wasn't

particularly friendly when he challenged Sydney after her opening remarks about the earlier Colorado case that seemed so per-
tinent to this one from New Jersey, if not dispositive.

Some of the Court members were elderly holdovers from
the decades-earlier crop of conservative Trump appointees, still
in the majority of the Court, but challenged recently by more
recent appointees of then Democratic President Julio Romero.
One of the elder justices jumped on Sydney soon after she began
her opening remarks.

"Counsel," began Justice Florida, a popular and genial conservative justice whose face reddened at any moment of anger
or humor, leading him to be facetiously labeled as a "small 'f'
Floridian," though he was from Ohio, "why shouldn't a genuinely religious person be assured the same respect of his good
faith personal views on religion, which also are protected by the
Constitution, as a gay couple whose sexual preferences might
offend the majority of people?"

Sydney knew she was in for a battle, and immediately cast
aside her prepared scholarly notes, and joined the true underlying social debate.

"Justice Florida," she looked up from her rostrum to make
eye contact, "thank you for directing our argument today to the
heart of what has been for many years a divisive issue in this
country."

Justice Florida interrupted, "And that would be?"

"That is, the strongly and genuinely conflicting views of some
Americans that their religious freedom is demeaned by part of the
community that snickers at their beliefs, and conflict with other
Americans whose equally personal views about same-sex marriage

are discriminated against by reactionary members of their home communities," Sydney responded. The issue was clearly joined.

The more moderate justice, former Minnesota Senator Amy Klobuchar, injected, "How would you have this Court strike a balance between these two competing values then, counselor?"

"By examining the underlying facts on a case by case basis," Sydney replied, "and determining them at the administrative hearing stage in these cases, which appellate courts rely on for the record of facts. The facts as much as the substantive issues will usually demonstrate whether a claim for religious protection is genuine, and based on individual conscience deserving of neutral protection, and whether the baker in this case in New Jersey provided equal services or products to heterosexual customers whose requests raised comparable design problems for the service provider. When the baker sold his cupcakes to any customer, he would not be assigned an artistic task which violated his religious principles."

"Such as?" Chief Justice Gordon Sanders interjected.

"Such as whether a gay school official refused to respect a hetero student's claim to be free from state demands of school administrators for student vaccinations due to their religious beliefs."

"Why shouldn't this Court uphold state restrictions if they are based on scientific conclusions, and be bound by our earlier bakery decision in 2018 in Colorado?" Justice Edith Sherman asked, changing the subject.

"Because," Sydney answered, "the Colorado civil rights commission found for the customers, the plaintiffs in that case, but this Court reversed it in favor of the baker's First Amendment free speech and religious rights. However, Colorado did not recognize gay marriage at that time. In New Jersey, gay marriage is now legal, so the competing interest of the lesbian customers is protected by the state, not like the baker in Colorado, as this Court ruled in that case."

Sydney was cooking now, she felt it and so did Ann who, smiling, looked back at their clients sitting nearby. If only the justices felt the game changing. No one would know that for months.

"What would your answer be to a claim of a philosophical principle that questioned public schools teaching the economic reasons for slavery, or some half-baked scholar denying the Holocaust?" Justice Irving Train asked.

This was going to be an ideological debate, not a coherent intellectual argument, Sydney realized, as she put aside her notes, straightened her back and fought on, ever so calmly for so contentious a conflict. Ann, at her side at the counsel table, realized what was happening, and shuffled Sydney's prepared notes to hand to her at appropriate moments.

"Thank you, Justice Train," Sydney replied. "One cannot use their religion or other honestly held beliefs to hurt other people because their offensive arguments—Holocaust denial, for example—are pseudo-intellectual and intended to be hurtful."

With every pause in the repartee with the justices, Sydney continued to make the points she intended to make, albeit in no rational order but in response to questions asked of her, or at pauses between questions the justices fired at her in no particular order of contested points. In response to a question reflecting one justice's sympathy with religious claims that the secular world thought were naïve or made in bad faith, Sydney switched from law professor to sympathetic common woman of the world.

"Perhaps some members of this Court saw one of my favorite movies, *Chariots of Fire*, which portrayed the conflict between the genuine claims of an Olympic runner that he could not run a race on the Sabbath, and the pressures of his church that he not make an exception, even in this unusual situation. Pressures on the runner nonetheless came from the Olympic Committee which needed his participation. 'I cannot make exceptions,' he told the Olympic Committee. 'When I run, I run for the pleasure of God.'"

"And what happened?" the non-movie-going justice inquired.

"The Committee compromised and he was assigned another day than Sunday to run. We all cheered, respecting his honest convictions, as we did in the Senate impeachment hearings of then President Trump, when then Senator Mitt Romney voted against the interest of his party's President, basing his difficult political decision on his devotion to his deep personal religious beliefs. Even the most cynical secularists applauded him for his bravery and integrity."

Back and forth the repartee continued until the fastest 30 minutes Sydney ever had lived passed, and the Chief Justice interrupted with a friendly, "Time's up, counselor."

As the next case, a prosaic patent matter, was called, and the lawyers for both sides shifted their papers and sat at the counsel tables, Sydney, Ann, and her clients left to attend televised interviews on the Court steps outside the building.

Partisans had arrived outside the Court at 5 a.m. to line up for seats when the case was called at 10 a.m. Some local Court watchers sold their spots to late arrivals as sometimes happens in notorious cases. Organized groups remained for the media cameras, some holding placards announcing their ideological sides. "If you don't sell us your cakes, we won't eat your cookies!" one set of signs proclaimed, while another stated: "Honor religion in schools, and marketplaces!" Opposing lawyers in the case made remarks too, but Sydney was played out by her 30 minutes wrestling with the canny justices, and was brief, not her best after the fact advocate.

That final task completed, the two lawyers and their clients returned to the inn on N Street for a celebratory lunch in its outdoor patio. Then, Sydney and Ann packed and taxied to Dulles Airport for their five-hour return flights—Sydney to San Francisco, Ann to San Diego.

*chapter 7*

# Emerson and Lehman, Together at Last

Sydney's victory in the wedding case put her on the go-to list for future women's groups precedential cases. Surprised by the Court's favorable decision, Sydney bragged she was undefeated— one for one at the Supreme Court. Not long after the decision, she got another call from Val at the Committee. This time it was to recruit Sydney in the appeal of a domestic violence case in Tampa, Florida, where it had been tried. The local counsel assigned by the court had not done a good job, to put it delicately, and the wife had been found guilty of first-degree murder. She had shot her violent husband who had repeatedly beaten her. But the jury— more than half were men—found her guilty, presumably because she had waited to act until her husband was asleep. Hours after her beating and her return home from her visit to the emergency room, she took his rifle and shot him three times.

When Sydney told Jake over dinner about her new assign-ment, she asked him if he would read the trial transcript and advise her on her brief to the appellate courts—whether she ignored any points in the trial record due to her never having tried a case. "Things like jury issues, judge rulings on evidence, prosecutorial misconduct," she explained. She'd handle the basic policy points in her brief and appellate argument, but she wanted to be sure that never having tried a criminal case, she wouldn't miss any points that should be raised.

Jake was pleased to be asked, said he wouldn't bill for his time reading the transcript and consulting with Sydney, and added sarcastically, "Now, you may even listen to me."

"I always listen," Sydney replied, "even if I don't agree with all your ideas."

"We're on the same side this time," Jake pointed out.

"Yes, the right side," she countered, continuing their friendly repartee.

When Jake read the transcript, he did have a few suggestions for Sydney. Apparently, Florida had no public defender system, so the court appointed a local favorite, despite the fact that he had never tried a capital case. He had urged his assigned client to accept a plea deal and plead guilty, in order to receive a maximum of 1–25 years in prison. His client wouldn't accept the deal because she couldn't leave her two young children (three and five years old) alone with the fractured family of her "monster" husband. Her attorney failed to call an expert witness to describe the awful PTSD victims suffer after their beatings in cases like this. The defendant testified that she and her alcoholic husband had an argument about some incidental household matter, and as he had done in the past, he called her a bitch, slugged her, and as she fought him off (she 5'4", 120 pounds; he 6'2", 210 pounds) her face was scratched, her skull was head-butted, and her arms and pelvic region were bruised badly by his crude beating.

Eventually, she fled the house and drove to a nearby hospital's emergency room, where doctors recorded and treated her injuries. When she returned, he was asleep, and after shooting him, she called 911.

When police arrived, she told them what had occurred and was arrested in front of her two young children. She was allowed to call her close friend to come and take her kids. The police took her to the local station where she was booked for murder in the first degree and denied bail, which meant that she would be separated from her children and jailed for months and unable to see her kids or assist in her defense.

Sydney knew from the women's group data that in recent years, women were incarcerated more than men in other situations, when they claimed to be acting appropriately when standing their ground. The Stand Your Ground defense was gaining application in domestic violence cases, however. She and Ann had included some of these cases in their book-to-be. But she was not so sure about appellate points that might be made by a savvy trial lawyer, and she lived with one!

Sydney was familiar with all the available data about Stand Your Ground laws in domestic violence cases. The Committee had provided her with sociological data about Tampa specifically and Florida generally that provided the background that might lead a local jury to convict this defendant even after seeing the E.R. report describing her injuries. The local DA used that evidence to demonstrate that the victim had been treated for her injuries before she shot her sleeping husband four hours after the "alleged" attack, demonstrating it was not a crime of passion or self-defense, but a planned, intended act not necessary for her safety when she "committed this deadly attack on her defenseless husband."

What Jake could add to Sydney's brief and argument were points even a law professor might miss if she had never tried a case. He was able to point out that the prosecutor used all his preemptive challenges to keep women off the jury, and that the judge did not, as he should have, instruct the jury that if it did not find the defendant guilty of premeditated murder, it could instead find her guilty of a lesser offense than first-degree murder, as an alternative to not guilty. He also suggested that Sydney point out that the defense counsel did not object to the DA prejudicially referring to the husband's brutal beating as merely "rough sex," dog whistling to the men on the jury how susceptible men in these parts were "to angry, retaliatory spouses these days."

By the time the appellate briefs were filed, and the Florida Supreme Court failed to find errors that might have reversed the jury's verdict, the case was appealed to the US Supreme Court by the Committee. Sydney was then the co-author of *the* book on gender law, Dean at Stanford Law, and might be able to boast that she was two for two in the US Supreme Court. She had added Jake's name to their brief, though he hadn't asked her to. He had collected enough courtroom victories on his own cases to be able to generously tell Sydney and their friends that "Emerson and Lehman were an unbeatable team." He did accompany Sydney to Washington, DC, to sit with her at counsel table. Along with several Committee members, their two young children had reserved seats to watch their mom in action (and their dad at her side).

The Supreme Court ultimately ruled their way, finding that the Florida Supreme Court gave too much weight to the trial court's rulings that were objected to (Jake's points) and found in favor of Sydney's argument that in view of all the errors, the case should be returned to the trial court for retrial, and the defendant released until that time from her already long incarceration. The local district attorney decided not to defend his predecessor (from another political party) and retry the case. It was then dismissed on the prevailing Allen case rule where a defendant could plead guilty to a lesser offense, thus avoiding the state being sued in civil court for its questionable years-long imprisonment for "the clearly battered wife," the new, more liberal DA mentioned.

Ann made sure the case was added to her and Sydney's manuscript. Jake's firm added it to his impressive list of Supreme Court victories.

*chapter 8*

# A Family Dilemma

For years, Sydney provided regular legal assistance for the five major national women's groups, writing amicus briefs in precedential cases, serving twice as counsel in Supreme Court arguments. After the New Jersey baker case, she had handled the domestic violence case. She was two for two. Occasionally, Sydney provided advisory talks on evolving legal issues of special interest to women.

The five separate organizations, Emily's List, Women's Legal Circle, Vota Latina, Alliance for Gender Justice, and NAACP's Women's Division would occasionally join efforts on subjects of common interest. They adopted a shorthand name, The Board, which met on special occasions warranting joint action when their special interests matched.

Sydney was not a political activist; she left politics to Jake and his work with Peter. She was a scholar, educator, writer, and a popular non-organizational women's leader, respected by all activist groups, but personally uninterested in politics.

She received a call at her office at Stanford from Val Peterson, Emily's List's veteran leader, saying the "The Board" was in Los Angeles for a few days of meetings. Could she meet with them for lunch one of those days? Sydney was always pleased to meet with these influential "players." They chose a date Sydney would be in Palo Alto; the trip costs to Los Angeles would be on them. Sydney guessed the subject that brought them together was important, as they met infrequently. Probably another Supreme Court test case she would be asked to handle or advise on, which she always enjoyed as a touch of reality to her academic life. Sydney discovered when she met her friends at the hotel where they were staying that the subject of the day was not academic.

When she arrived at the Luxe Hotel, she was directed to one of the suites her colleagues had reserved as their informal work site. With Val was Rachel Greenberg, director of Women's Legal Circle, a litigation organization based in Washington, DC; Flo Esposito from Vota Latina in LA; Nancy Trynin of Alliance for Gender Justice, an umbrella organization of 130 special interest organizations based in New York City, representing gay and lesbian, business, and media organizations; and Eleanor Jordan from NAACP's Women's Division in Chicago. In the suite were tables filled with trays of food; other tables were covered with papers and files. The five board members rose in unison to greet Sydney when she arrived. After a brief friendly catch up, Val interrupted the friendly chatter.

"Sydney," she said, "we are so pleased you could meet with us on short notice on the important matter that brings us together. Let me not waste one minute of all our time to delay telling you why we wanted to meet with you."

The other attendees and Sydney sat as Val continued, "You know, of course, that Elena has been hospitalized, again." First names were used even in august meetings, including Supreme Court justices known personally to all present. Their board predecessors had championed Kagan's academic rise to Dean of

Harvard Law School years ago, and later to Solicitor General in the Department of Justice, and then her elevation to Associate Justice. Now past 80, Kagan had endured a series of operations, and there was speculation about whether and when she might retire. The Board wanted to be sure they had the right replacement.

"Sydney, we all feel you are the perfect one, and we want to discuss Kagan's replacement with you privately before it becomes a public affair. We have a year before the election and are more comfortable with the politics of Elena's eventual replacement under the present administration."

There was silence as all eyes turned toward Sydney. She was stunned for a moment. Then, she replied, "I'm flattered by your compliment, of course. May I have a few days to think about this surprise? Please don't think I am blasé about this amazing offer. It's just that I am so settled in California, my kids are now out of the house at colleges, and Jake and I are living the wonderful life of empty-nesters. Plus, I just finished my five-year term as Dean and have embraced a cozy life of teaching and writing at Stanford for life." Sydney paused a moment. "You must think me crazy not to leap at your offer. I just need time to process what you have said."

Rachel jumped in. "Of course you should take the time you need, but as an old professor once said to me, take your time dear, but be quick about it." Laughs resounded from the group.

"Of course you will want to discuss this idea with your family, the law school," Flo added. "Would our next conference work for you? That is in two weeks in Washington. We want you, unanimously, but need to begin the process of readying our candidate, you we hope, for the initiation to the preparation that goes with this media show, and confirmation hearings. With your academic reputation, we think the noise of past contentious confirmation hearings should be minimal. And having clerked on the Court—a Republican one, at that—makes you a perfect, non-political candidate."

Sydney didn't remember much more of the conversation, so many thoughts raced in her mind. Moving back to DC after all these years. What would Jake do? The kids were in college so it didn't matter where they visited on holidays.

All else faded as old professional colleagues had lunch, gossiped about people and events they all cared about. A few hours later, Sydney was on a plane returning to San Francisco. She called Jake with the exciting news from the airport, promising to fill him in on all the details later that evening when they would be together.

▥

It didn't take long to find out. There are supposed to be no coincidences in life. But a classic puzzler was about to happen.

Peter and Jake met regularly at Peter's club for friendly business and social and political conversations. That afternoon, Peter returned from a political meeting in Washington, DC, and called Jake to invite him for a drink at his home for "some very exciting news." Jake assumed something hot was brewing.

"What's up," Jake asked when he arrived, "that you were so hush-hush about? You sure have my curiosity meter tweaked."

Peter poured each of them their favorite pre-dinner drinks. "Jake, I just came from the Democratic National Committee meeting in Washington. When the subject of the President's imminent Supreme Court appointment to replace the expected retirement of Justice Kagan came up, I tossed your name out and got a very positive reaction."

Peter smiled, handed Jake his drink, and sat down across from him, expecting some expression of joy from his friend and long-time counsel.

Instead, Jake looked shocked, said nothing for some moments.

"What's the matter?" Peter asked. "We are talking about you returning to the Court you clerked in years ago. What an accomplishment! Why the look of shock?"

Jake finally responded, "I'm sorry, Peter, of course that was a huge compliment, what you did, and ordinarily I, anyone, would jump for joy. What you don't know is that I just learned that Emily's List and a group of influential national women's organizations are supporting Sydney for the seat. I am a competitive guy, but the last person I would push ahead of in any line is my wife!"

"Ouch!" Peter reacted. "Life *is* complicated. I am *so* sorry that what was meant as great news, isn't. What do we do now?"

"I don't know, and I don't mean to be ungrateful for your friendship and help, after all these years. Let me think about this, talk to Syd when she gets home tonight, and get back to you. I need to think about this after she and I talk. But I always will remember you for this act, and love you for it."

"Well," Peter said as he saw Jake out of his house, "do think about it. Of course, discuss it with Sydney. My consolation may be to have you here where I appreciate your friendship, and always need your sage counsel."

Jake went home that night full of anxiety and confusion, not what others would be thinking after learning such exciting news. Maybe he could stand back now and ask Peter if the offer would hold until the next opening of a seat on the Court.

In fact, it didn't take long for Jake to conclude that there really was no quandary. Sydney should have her shot at the new seat on the Court, given that her career at Stanford had already reached its summit, and her current age left her time for another historic career. Jake knew by the time he returned home that evening what he must do. As soon as he arrived, he went upstairs to his home office and called Peter.

"Peter, Jake. Listen, my dear friend. I must ask you to take my name off this list. I can't be a factor in Syd's shot at being on the Supreme Court. I'll always love you for your long support of me. Who knows, maybe someday Syd and I can manage what Rehnquist and O'Connor didn't." Jake recalled hearing an NPR story years before about the late Chief Justice William Rehnquist's college courtship in 1949 at Stanford Law School with his then fellow student and future Supreme Court colleague Justice Sandra Day O'Connor, to whom he was reported to have proposed marriage. Their personal relationship might have led to heated debates if that happened, when she was later nominated to the same Court as her husband then headed. The courtship never concluded and they remained friends, married to others. Better that issue, pillow talk at the Supreme Court, had come up before. His and Sydney's marriage would raise recusal questions when he had a case before the Court, but that should not necessarily create a quandary.

His worry now was how to balance his life with Sydney

somewhere else most of the year. Aware of the dated practice of wives usually following husbands in the work world, Jake concluded, "I have to reverse the precedent, one Sydney has always championed. I'm not going to tell her about your good will attempt, so don't mention it to Marie. Our next dinner is on me. Stay close, my friend. I may be a lonely bachelor if Sydney goes to Washington."

"No good deed goes unpunished," Peter thought to himself. That worldly aphorism led to Sydney's and Jake's brouhaha that followed both of their separate conversations with their fan clubs and Court sponsors.

After Jake's call, Peter let his colleagues at the DNC know that Jake would be supporting Sydney and asked to be struck from the list, but to pass on his sincere thanks for their consideration. Jake hadn't told Sydney when she called, as he thought the potential conflict was avoided. But Sydney's sponsors had heard that Jake's name was on the DNC list and called her private cell phone to ask if she knew. She didn't. And that thought annoyed her on her now anxious return home from Los Angeles.

Shortly after Jake arrived, Sydney rushed into the house and blurted out, "Why didn't you tell me?"

Jake thought she was referring to his instruction to Peter to take his name off the list which he didn't want her to know. "There was nothing to tell, babe, you know I'm the president of your fan club."

"Some fan club, babe yourself, I can't believe you'd do this to me."

Now Jake was understandably miffed at Sydney's accusation. "Do exactly *what* to you?"

"Don't play dumb with me," Sydney replied accusingly. "I always knew you and I had different views about gender, but I believed even you would not attempt to eclipse my candidacy!"

"Even me!" Jake was abashed.

Jake was so upset, he screamed, "What are you talking about? Is there is no way to please you?" and blasted out of their house, slamming the front door.

Jake drove back to his office to distract himself from his wife's rancor by working late into the evening, then stopping off late at a local pub to drown his sorrows. He so drowned them that he took a cab home when the friendly bartender suggested he leave his car in the garage and called him a taxi. Jake entered quietly, and dropped half-dressed onto their living room couch and fell into a hard sleep in the living room.

Morning arrived, brutally.

Jake awoke hurting from his hard night's sleep and aching head, and went upstairs to shower and decide how to continue the bracing day. No doubt, Sydney was still pissed off. And so was he. Their family seemed to be coming apart.

Sydney answered the family phone when it rang. It was Val. "Wow, what a husband you have, Syd!"

Sydney was confused, thinking Val was calling to share her disappointment. "Yeah, what a guy! Sometimes you don't know who your friends are. I am crushed. And embarrassed."

Val couldn't understand the conversation and asked, "Am I missing something, or didn't Jake decline to be a candidate to make way for you?" Suddenly Sydney was silent, guilt-ridden, aware she had made a big mistake: an unforgivable one. "Val, I misunderstood. Thanks for calling. I must run, but I will call you back soon."

Sydney rushed upstairs where she found Jake dressing, look-ing sullen, standing silent as she entered.

Now Jake was confused as Sydney took him into her arms, weeping, kissing his neck, shamefully apologizing. "How could I have underestimated you, Jake? Can you ever forgive me? You should have told me."

Jake could feel her wet tears on his neck as Sydney embraced him. He began to understand how they had been two ships passing in a night of misperception. He stood back, and looked arm's-length at Sydney. "Syd, I'm a trial lawyer. I'd rather argue cases than judge them. Even so, how could you imagine that I would compete with you—you're so obviously the right choice!"

Sydney embraced Jake again, crying into his face. "Oh, Jake, forgive me, please."

"Nothing to forgive, love, only a life to reassemble so you can make history."

*chapter 9*

# Welcome to the Circus

When, as expected, Elena Kagan died, Sydney soon got the word that meetings had been set up at the White House with lawyers who would prep her for the imminently scheduled Senate hearings to confirm her appointment by the President. She should plan on a week in Washington, DC, where she would be introduced to key senators on the Judiciary Committee between "dry runs" under the tutelage and questioning of veteran legislative counsel at the White House, and receive advice from PR folks to "suggest stylistic outfits for her dress-up at the Senate televised hearings," and from speech coaches to ready her for her prospective answers to the questioning by the senators. She would be thoroughly brainwashed.

Sydney had looked forward to her debut as a public figure and liked the idea that she was being offered "advice" about the important process she'd be a key part of, until she arrived to undergo what she later told Val and Jake was "the worst week of my life."

Sydney arrived, ready to work and eager to enter her new life-to-be. She was provided quarters at the Hay-Adams hotel directly across from the White House, where she would sleep, and not much else. Stealthily, she would be picked up at 9 a.m. by her secret service escorts of the week, who never left her side.

Briefings took place in the adjoining Executive Office Building next to the White House, in cavernous rooms with old-fashioned chandeliers lighting a capacious space, several unused fireplaces, and a table long enough for a plane to land on covered daily with briefing books and files, alongside a perpetually refilled side table with coffee, water, sweet rolls, sandwiches—enough to feed a corps of soldiers. They lived in that room all week, interrupted only by visits to senators that were set up steadily but scheduled when Senate staffers called the group to say, "Senator so-and-so will see Professor Emerson between 4:00 and 4:15." Then they'd return to the crash course for Sydney's interviews. They worked at the Executive Office meeting room until around 9:30 p.m., when her manager would stand up and announce, "Good day, all. Professor, you must be tired. We'll escort you back to the hotel, and pick up where we left off, bright and early. You'll be picked up tomorrow at 9."

After day one, it wasn't fun. She would return to her hotel room exhausted, undress hurriedly, and fall asleep immediately. Then she would awake and go through a similar routine the next day. And the next. Val would meet her sometimes at the Hay-Adams for a quick breakfast in Sydney's room (no public appearances that might get media attention). The only photos of Sydney from that seemingly month-long week was of her walking across Lafayette Park to the White House, accompanied by her two secret service guards, tailed by a morning pack of sleepy-eyed camera men and women, shouting entreaties to their uncommunicating prey.

On the landing strip table, where she found herself seated most of the time, were reams of tax returns; FBI reports; press clippings; articles she wrote or was quoted in; high school, college, and grad school records; exams she took; every word she ever wrote; and TV clips of all her public appearances. Her mentors had gathered just about every record of her life, including medical records she'd been asked to provide (probably against the law of privacy) and explain. It was mortifying—a potential Supreme Court Justice for life being treated like a war prisoner by young, over-earnest lawyers. Proper always, while always probing. Sydney wondered when she'd be asked to strip off her clothes to be examined by Nurse Ratched.

Sydney understood that the confirmation process in the Senate was not the historical courtesy call of the past that took a few respectful hours and disclosed nothing contentious or controversial. Ever since the notorious Robert Bork, Clarence Thomas, and Brett Kavanaugh hearings, the White House and Senate staff lawyers scripted a play. The witness appointee, accompanied by a phalanx of lawyers and crews of photographers, entered the formal hearing room with his or her adoring family. Sydney took lobs from friendly senators prepped to make her attendance easy, and hostile examinations from the other political side (the minority of the Committee used the televised hearings to impress the voters back home, and show off their theatrical talents, such as they were).

The arranged meetings with key senators prior to her appearance were brief, perfunctory, staged, with an occasional old goat senator in his office trying for a peek up Sydney's dress (soon to be replaced by dark slacks). Sydney learned the whole circus was to avoid surprises, or controversial repartees (as the earlier Chief Justice John Roberts classically mis-described his prospective role as simply an "umpire calling balls and strikes," rather than the real truth that, as the adage goes, "the law is what the Justices say it is").

When it all ended, Sydney returned to California, exhausted, cynical, but hopeful that her hell week would be followed by most lawyers' lifetime dream job.

▥

At the hearings, six weeks later. Jake and their two children who came this time were coached by Sydney's managers where to be, how to appear, and never to speak, except Jake who could reply to questions, "We're so proud of Sydney; she's the perfect choice for this job."

The hearing room was packed. A thousand cameras, or so it appeared, clicked away from the moment the entourage entered the hearing room, and continued while Sydney spoke, disconcerted by the clickety-clack which interfered with her concentration on the senators' questions. Her friendly senators were courtly and threw softballs at her, posing such probing questions as, "Professor Emerson, do you believe in *stare decisis*, in cases where you disagree with the precedent in question?" Hostile senators threw fastballs, as close to Sydney's head as they dared. "Professor, what is your position on the murder of fetuses in abortion? Should that be prosecuted as a crime?" Each in the latter group hoped for a quotable jab that might make the evening news clips of the hearings.

Sydney was proper and smarter by far than her questioners on the work of the Supreme Court and the hot button legal issues which divided her country. Her hearings concluded when all the Committee members had their on-camera moments. That night, Sydney declined her team's offer for dinner at the White House visitors dining room, preferring a private dinner with Jake, Maria, and Richard at the Hay-Adams's refined, decorous, quiet, and half-empty dining room.

After showering and changing clothes and packing for their return flight to California the next morning, the four of them had dinner at the dining room downstairs. After their orders were taken, Maria said, "Mom, we were proud of you today." Sydney smiled and nodded thanks.

Richard joked, "I don't envy you living with those eight old fogies wearing robes all the time. Where are their wigs?"

Jake finally lifted his glass of wine and toasted Sydney seriously. "My love, when we came to Washington as kids, and fell in love, we didn't really know where we'd end up. Stanford, for you maybe. Us together was all I cared about. How wonderful it is, and how proud you must be to be back where you began professionally. Your first job is now your lifelong work. Your accomplishment is for the history books. Congratulations, my love."

"Ahhh," both children sighed.

The next day, all four flew home to San Francisco, now their former home. A month later, when her nomination was approved by the Senate, Sydney (accompanied by her family, again mostly silent in Christmas-card-like poses) was sworn in, hand on her old family bible at the White House held by the aged Justice

Neil Gorsuch, the last member of the Court who was a justice when Sydney and Jake had served as clerks. The smiling President looked on, as did her eight future colleagues on the Court.

Another chapter of their exciting life began then.

*chapter 10*

# An Innocent Moment

Marriages, even the best of them, can become rote, habitual more than exciting. But for Sydney and Jake, theirs took on the sense of a second honeymoon. They wanted to be with each other more and didn't want separation to characterize their future.

Logistics were necessary. Sydney would be in Washington. Jake was with her some of those times as they planned their moves from one big family house in California to two small but elegant condo apartments in DC and San Francisco. Sydney would reside most of the time in DC, Jake in San Francisco. For vacations and summer breaks, Sydney would be in San Francisco with Jake. No one stayed in Washington in the summer if they didn't have to.

When the Court was in session, Jake would come to DC for special events that included spouses, or when he had firm business there. His firm was amenable to his leading a new satellite office in the nation's capital. In fact, the social columns in San Francisco and DC often mentioned the comings and goings of the young-"ish," attractive, bicoastal couple. Sydney devoted her time in Washington to hard work on Court matters like she did when she was a clerk. In California, Jake was a workaholic, partially to deflect loneliness, partially to be assured there would be time with Sydney when that was possible. When he was alone, his firm colleagues were socially inclusive to the point of exhausting a grateful Jake, who preferred some quiet, private time.

Peter, as always, included Jake in his life, both professionally and socially. But, bottom line, Sydney and Jake missed each other in all their mundane daily routines. They talked by phone in separate beds following the time zone difference to make their calls possible. Each had much to tell the other on their long calls about their lives apart. But for the fact they had children, elsewhere mostly, it was like their clerkship days when work took up their time but distance actually brought back romance, at least a middle-aged variety. They were farther away from each other than ever before but deeply connected whenever there were moments to connect.

But "helpful" friends couldn't resist intruding in their very public lives, wondering, "How could their perfect marriage last?" when they were apart most of the time.

Later, there came a time in the splendid script of the Sydney–Jake perfect life story when everything seemed to go awry. Sydney was becoming a force on the Court and a star in Washington society. Jake was practicing in San Francisco when he was there, was a favored guest at every party and event, and he was always available for dinner parties and tickets available last minute in his days alone. He loved being part of Sydney's life when he was with her in DC, as she did when she was with Jake in San Francisco. It was that perfect life that gave rise to questions they never had faced.

Ed Vector and Sydney exchanged Christmas cards through the years, those common "Here's the latest picture of the baby, this year we went to Yosemite, Caron has braces" letters we all receive from old friends we never see now, but hear from annually. Recent ones mentioned Ed's divorce, "life goes on," and the latest announced that "now that the kids are away in school," Ed was coming to join the Corps of Engineers in Washington, DC, to "change the scene" and make a fresh start in his life. Not long after Sydney returned to Washington, Ed arrived to start his new life. It was natural and welcome company for them to have occasional dinners when their schedules allowed. Nothing more. Though skeptics wondered, privately.

Gina Singh was one of Jake's partners at Brock and Arguello, with whom he had worked successfully on several appellate matters. She was very bright (born and educated in the U.K.), attractive, divorced, dating perfunctorily, and seemed to be independent. Sydney knew and liked Gina and was pleased Jake had in her a colleague with no social commitments and as such a likely arms-length friend to him, to them. Firm colleagues suspected nothing gossipy about them and their work, even their occasional trips together. There was some infrequent winking mention of them (behind their backs they were referred to as Singh and Dance), but nothing widespread nor serious. Both were well liked by their colleagues at Brock and Arguello.

Nothing is innocent in smarmy eyes, so there were occasional whispers when Sydney showed up at an event in Washington with Ed, or when Jake was seen at a San Francisco dinner party or the ballet with Gina. Neither Sydney nor Jake were aware of those whispers, as in their innocent eyes there was nothing to be aware of.

The first eager slander from a "friend" jealous of Sydney's and Jake's seemingly perfect life happened when Jake was asked by an acquaintance during one of his business trips to Washington, "Wasn't it nice that Sydney had Ed's company on some of her required events?" Jake nodded "yes," remarking that they are old high school friends, and he thought nothing of it. Juniors at the firm who really did not know Jake or Sydney wondered, gossiping over lunch, if Jake and Gina were "an item." Marie even asked Peter if it wasn't odd that Jake used their tickets to the opera to escort Gina one evening. Their seatmates made a juicy remark to Marie about Jake's exotic-looking date that planted an idea she found hard to believe. Peter did ask Jake, nonchalantly, "Who did you take to *Tosca*?"

"One of my B&A colleagues, Gina Singh," Jake replied. "She handles our international business. Loves opera, knows all the music."

What made the "problem" surface was a result of fortuity and how virtuous paths can suggest worse results than unvirtuous ones.

Sydney spent the summer months in San Francisco with Jake, working at home on her pending cases and sharing an occasional weeknd visiting vineyards with him, while Jake continued his work at his firm. One weekend, Jake and Gina attended a high-level conference sponsored by The State Trial Judges Association in Sacramento on "New Guidelines for Appellate Practice." As leading advocates in California, they had a prominent role at the conference, and their panels were heavily attended by colleagues in their field from around the country. It really was a working conference, not the boondoggle some summer events for professionals are: breakfast, one panel, golf, lunch, separate meetings, golf, and a winey dinner to share war stories from their firm practices.

After one of their dinners in Sacramento, feeling the effects of their alcoholic rewards for exacting efforts that day, attendees returned to their rooms late. Jake had just undressed when he received a call from Gina, with whom he would co-chair a panel the next day.

"Sorry to call so late," Gina said. "I just heard from Eliot Wise. He has food poisoning and doubts he can be on our panel in the morning. Any ideas how we fill in for him?"

"Do you have the panel papers?" Jake asked. "This was one you arranged."

"Yes, but if you could spare a few minutes, perhaps an early breakfast, help brainstorm with me about who could fill in. You know these characters and their specialties better than I, and I would be relieved."

"Let me come by now, and see what you have. Breakfast may be too late to fill our hole and find a replacement."

Jake pulled on his informal outfit (slacks and a golf shirt), and dashed to Gina's room down the hall. When he arrived, Gina was the opposite of her usual carefully dressed, properly groomed self, in a bathrobe, no shoes, flustered by the problem at hand. Jake looked over her files, saw one listed person who he knew and thought would be an appropriate last minute replacement. Jake took Gina's file and as he left she hugged him, impetuously, stepped back undone by her awkwardness, and looked at him saying, "I'm so sorry, Jake."

They looked at each other for a moment, aware that this quite personal contact was unusual, wondering momentarily whether in another time and place lines might have been crossed that weren't. Each was embarrassed, even tempted, but their virtue remained intact. They shared a moment of awareness of intimacy, desire, temptation, and resistance they each realized was present in the room.

It was only a split second, but Gina and Jake were aware of each other in a way they'd not experienced in years of professional and informal social dealings. Gina was always dressed formally, stylishly; here, she was covered but undressed and Jake could see and feel her figure, soft and natural under her robe. Gina could sense Jake too, himself not costumed formally this time as he was in all others. Jake could smell Gina, not her subtle perfumed public scent but her real, personal one. With her makeup off and no high-heeled shoes, Gina was shorter than Jake had seen her, softer, too, more human than he imagined. They had been at arm's length from each other for so long that at that instant they felt a strange, personal connection that startled them as they stepped away. As Jake left, they looked at each other and saw themselves as they had not before, and their minds and imaginations soared.

"Good night, Gina, I'll meet you at breakfast. Meanwhile, I'll try to call Bill Lynch and see if I can recruit him as our relief pitcher. He'd be perfect," Jake said quietly as he walked with his head down out of Gina's room.

He didn't notice Judge Emily Henderson entering her room nearby as he exited Gina's room, preoccupied as he was by his new chore and his strangely guilty feelings about his recent encounter.

*chapter 11*

# Never A Dull Moment

If there were questions about Sydney and Ed Vector, they were few and were left unanswered. Supreme Court Justices having active sex lives was like thinking about your parents having sex. Easy to put out of one's mind. It was moot anyway because Ed was now regularly seen with a lady he'd met at work, though he and Sydney continued their occasional friendship.

The whispers about Jake and Gina, however, persisted—to both of their embarrassments. It resulted in Jake losing a friend with whom he'd had good times, without crossing lines they'd both only thought about in their one ambiguous moment. It wasn't ambiguous to Judge Henderson, who "discretely" asked some friends and colleagues about their views of Jake and Gina. They, of course, "discretely" asked some of their close friends, and the rumor spread like a social virus. No one directly mentioned the matter to Jake or Gina, but they had heard about it and chose to ignore it. They did, however, back away from most of their out-of-office engagements.

On one of Jake's trips with Peter to the DNC, they discussed the upcoming presidential convention and the rules that would prevail. Jake was counsel to the Committee and loved the excuse to be with Sydney in Washington.

As one of the meetings broke up and small groups departed or reconvened, Jake and Peter were pulled to the side of the room by another power broker on the DNC, Gabriel Rizzo, a New Jersey politician who knew Peter, liked him, and had a secretive suggestion.

"Let me buy you two a drink, downstairs at the club bar," Gabe whispered, taking each by the arm and gently steering them to a more private chat elsewhere. It was early for a drink, 4:30, and there would be a formal business dinner at seven that Peter would attend with the other DNC members. Jake reserved that open time for him to meet Sydney at a restaurant located midway between both their offices.

When the three were seated in a corner of the half empty pub, Gabe told Peter and Jake what was on his mind. "I've got good news and one piece of bad news I want to discuss with both of you," he began.

"And what mysterious plot are you about to present, Gabe?" Peter asked, smiling.

"The word is out that Chief Justice Sanders is about to retire. The President plans to move up Troy Jones, to be the first black Chief Justice. That will leave Jones's seat open— he's from Newark so this is how I know about all this, from a hush hush White House meeting with Jonesy and others. I know Peter wanted your name presented last time there was an opening, and I understand you preferred to not compete with your wife and told Peter to pull your name from consideration— not many people would act as nobly. But my question is, do we make history by appointing Jake here, and have the first spousal couple on the Court?"

Jake couldn't wait to tell Sydney the news. They met at Drake's, their place to celebrate good news in their old clerking days. When they met, were seated, and ordered drinks, Sydney said, "You seem in another place. What's up?"

"You're not going to believe this, and you can't talk about it, either. It may not happen anyway . . ." Jake bumbled along in a way Sydney had never witnessed.

"Get to it, Jake," she interrupted. "What's your story?"

"My story is . . . you may know this . . ."

"Know what? Out with it!"

"I learned at our DNC meeting today that the Chief Justice is about to retire, and his replacement may be Troy Jones."

"That trial balloon is known," Sydney replied. "What's the news?"

"The news is . . . I've been asked if I want my hat tossed into the ring to replace Troy!"

Sydney stared at Jake, silently. Eventually, she loudly, happily blurted out, "Jake, I can't believe this!" causing heads to turn at nearby tables.

"I'm so glad you are so discrete, and can keep a secret," Jake kidded.

The rest of their dinner, and in bed at Sydney's apartment later that evening, their conversation about Jake's news continued.

When will it be public? Is it definite? Can we tell the kids?

Will my being on the Court be a complication? A plus? Or a minus?

"Thanks for clearing things up," Jake responded. "I don't have answers to any of your questions. And no one, not even our kids, can know. There are too many question marks. I was asked if I wanted the job, and said, 'Are you kidding?' But it's in the lap of the gods. Maybe the President has someone else in mind. Maybe it would be too risky to nominate the spouse of a sitting Justice, for the first time, at that."

It was a long time before Sydney and Jake fell asleep that night, and Jake was scheduled to fly back to San Francisco the following day. The excited couple had breakfast together; then, Sydney was off to the Court, and Jake to meet Peter for the Committee's last meetings. It would take time before any of their questions would be answered.

Jake, Peter, and Gabe met together over lunch later that day, and Peter had included Ed Woodson from Maine and Victor Marcus of Chicago, two influential fellow committee members he had recruited to their cabal to discuss yesterday's report by Gabe.

When they were seated, each of them were conscious of the need to meet privately and talk fast as each had a plane to catch. After Gabe opened the discussion, Jake interrupted. "You said last night you had good news and some bad news," he stated. "You told me the good, but we were so excited, I never asked you what the bad news was."

Gabe answered, "That's one of the things we need to discuss, and Ed and Victor here will jump in with their questions."

"Let's get on with it," Jake said.

"Ok," Gabe responded, "the good news is that I was asked

by Peter about my feelings about your nomination, and I'm all for it. Any ghosts in the closet I should know about?" he asked. "Peter, you need to raise this one matter, confidential between friends and supporters."

"Jake," Peter now added, "this nomination and confirmation process can be nasty."

"You're telling me," Jake interrupted. "The prep alone was the worst week of Sydney's life, she told me."

"And she really had no opposition," Gabe noted. "I hope that's the case with you. I have no reason to question that, but we need an answer to Peter's story."

Peter jumped in, "Jake you know my feelings about you and Sydney, and under no other circumstances would I have raised this question with you." Peter stopped a moment. "But I am aware of scuttlebutt back home that, between you and me, I'm concerned about. It's plain rumor and not worth repeating. But if there's anything to it, we'll need to deal with it, privately now, in case we have to publicly later." Peter paused.

"What the hell are you referring to, Peter?" Jake asked.

Peter continued, "It has to do with your relationship with Gina."

"What relationship?" Jake interrupted. "She's my colleague at Brock and Arguello. Everyone knows that."

"But the rumor is—this is me being candid as your friend, I'd never repeat this any other time—but . . . Jake, did you and Gina have a personal affair?"

"Peter, how could you even suggest such a thing? Where did this slander come from? Gina and I are friends, colleagues. Period!"

"I know, I know," Peter responded. "I hate being the one

to tell you this. But if I heard the rumor, and I'm your friend, others must know it, and I'd never want you or Sydney to be publicly embarrassed."

Their two colleagues entered the conversation. "No one nowadays doesn't have some accusation like this abroad. When someone becomes a public figure, the rats come up the alley, and the media is there to give 'em a moment in the news. Once the news is out, the damage is done, and the accused is never looked at the same way again," Ed Woodson advised.

"So what do we do about it?" Jake asked.

"Nothing," Peter interrupted. "Since there is no fire—and I totally believe if Jake says so that there is none—we pray no currency is given to such a rumor, confident that Gina will support you, Jake, if somehow it did come out."

"Of course," Jake answered, "there is nothing to this cheap gossip."

For a minute, there was silence around the table. Diplomatically as possible under the circumstance, the three Committee colleagues ended the conversation. "If there is no risk, we can't worry, and we sue the shit out of any public mention of the scurrilous charge."

The only one still worried about that happening was Jake. He remembered the late night he and Gina had met in her hotel room to discuss replacing a panelist. But he couldn't bear this unfounded story being made public. What would Sydney think? Their kids? The firm? Why is it the scurrilous don't worry and get NDAs hiding the truth, and he, totally innocent, shocked to learn the false story, feels awful?

"It isn't fair," Gabe said. "JFK, Clinton, and Trump ran

around shamelessly, and they got elected President of the United States, for Chrissake. I know one really nice businessman who never cheated, was blackmailed by a harridan temp secretary, and eventually committed suicide. Don't let it get to you, Jake, this is the big leagues and the play can be rough."

Jake knew about the stressful next steps because he'd vicariously lived through Sydney's nomination and confirmation. This time, however, there was an additional hurdle: if confirmed, this would be the first time ever that a husband and wife would be members of the Supreme Court. The President's insider friends provided mixed advice. On the subject of political correctness, now there were three women including Sydney, and a new black justice (the President would be the first to promote one to Chief Justice). Was it time to appoint a gay, Hispanic, or disabled lawyer? Jake was more middle-of-the-road, just a standard white male; would the correctness critics complain?

"That again?" one young advisor wondered.

"Well, he *is* Jewish," another pointed out.

What Jake had going for him was that the women's groups remembered Jake's sensitivity when he declined to run against Sydney when she was nominated. For sure they liked the potential optics of a woman Justice swearing in a man—her man, and junior to him on the Court, at that. This chip hadn't even been played before in the now theatrical game of "what's the novelty?"

Peter's role on the DNC helped too. He was a veteran in the party's power elite; he adored Jake, and he was owed chips by his colleagues for his past collegiality when they had a favor to ask or a favorite candidate to promote. "We need a second westerner, too, don't we?" one poohbah reminded the selection advisory committee. Sydney was the only other, and in addition, Jake didn't have an Ivy League background like most justices.

So Mr. Vanilla, as one sarcastic critic labelled Jake, went through the back-room, insider poker game with little competition. Even the planning process Sydney hated was easier for Jake. Both California Senators were influential, and they knew and liked Jake from his political work as Peter's man. His confirmation was an example of how it used to be. There was one exception which Jake used to demonstrate his sense of humor, that turned a potential tense moment into a light one. One senator from the opposition, known to be a hostile if not provocative questioner, asked Jake a question.

"Mr. Lehman," Senator Tommie Harper, known informally as Tommy the harpooner, asked, "in just about every case that comes before the Court, does your wife, Justice Emerson, the author of this notable book *Recusal*," he lifted a copy to make his sarcastic point, "have to recuse herself for a conflict if you disagree?"

There was a moment when the attending media looked up, attentive, expecting some hostility to emerge. But Jake was ready for the question, having tried several cases already before the Court while Sydney was a justice.

"You ask a pungent question, Senator," he responded. "That question never arose in the four cases I argued before the Court while Justice Emerson sat as a justice. In fact, some sarcastic reporters mentioned at the time the irony when she voted against my client's interest. Friends who know us, and are aware of Justice Emerson's independence, may have wondered if this factor might indeed prejudice my clients."

Some in the audience in attendance could be heard laughing, and even Senator Harper enjoyed the clever repartee that answered the question in a way he could only smile at.

His mother (his father had died) and two children, and Sydney, of course, made the perfect photo backdrop at the Senate hearing. The confirmation vote was a uniquely bipartisan 78–22. And the media loved the married justices spin, and they all spun it.

In fact, Court watchers, aware of Sydney's earlier book *Recusal*, referenced Senator Harper's question, by remarking on the subject of recusal generally. Most commentators took the position that her widely respected book had led to reforms of the applicable law of recusal so that any questioned justice now had clear guidelines on what was a proper ground for seeking to recuse, and provided an appeal of any justice's decision not to recuse themself if the justice did not have an acceptable reason to do so.

The debate appeared to slough the potentially awkward subject of matrimonial responsibilities generally, particularly among married observers. Sydney and Jake and his managers at the hearings were relieved that this potentially embarrassing issue became moot at this point.

What never surfaced was the Jake–Gina rumor. Peter had handled it deftly. His choice appointee as US Attorney in San Francisco "coincidentally" bumped into Gina on the street and chatted with her, briefly and off the record. When his touchy question came up, Gina literally stopped in the middle of the street, exclaiming, "What?" The courtly U.S. attorney took her arm gingerly and they continued their impromptu stroll. He told Gina he expected her reaction, had given no notice to the rumor, and she agreed before they parted to sign his proposed, already notarized affidavit stating succinctly and not self-defensively that Jake's work at Brock and Arguello, as all their colleagues confirmed, was as a trusted professional, and they all admired the perfect personal partnership Jake and Sydney epitomized.

"Thank you, Gina. I was sure that would be the case, and I expect it will never be needed." It wasn't.

All their prior clerk colleagues were photographed at Jake's swearing in by the Chief Justice and the President. Begowned Sydney held her old family heirloom bible—the New Testament version, at that.

"They're Back Again," proclaimed a Washington Post headline. The new glamorous couple were fodder for the media. And all the publicity was favorable, mostly personal and not jurisprudential.

Their lives in the academic world and the legal one, even working at the Supreme Court, didn't prepare Sydney and Jake for the networks' greetings to them in their new life. All of a sudden, the newly ordained hot DC couple who were not late-night television watchers started getting calls from friends.

"Sydney, did you see Trevor Jones last night?" one friend asked.

"Last night he did a riff on you and Jake," her pal reported.

"So, at the US Supreme Court yesterday, rookie Justice Jacob Lehman was observed leaving the courtroom with the other justices, heading through the curtains to their inner sanctum. He was seen surreptitiously patting the behind of one of his colleagues! Better be Justice Emerson, or there will be trouble under the robes tonight!"

Another late-night show host joked, a friend reported, that the new justices were overheard by a staff member at their first lunch date at the justice's dining room.

"What do I call you now?" Sydney asked.

"How about Justice Lehman around the Court," Jake reportedly answered. "Still lover in private."

"OK, lover boy, but at home, you still take out the garbage, as the newest Court member," his wife and colleague responded, as their waiter's head turned.

The networks seemed to jump onto the Supreme Court couple like metal chips to a magnet. On NBC, the anchor joked, "Last night, Supreme Court Justice Sydney Emerson was overheard talking to her justice hubby at a judicial conference held at the Mayflower Hotel."

"I dissent!" she exclaimed at the bar when her junior member husband, smiling slyly, said, "Isn't it time we returned to our apartment, honey? Honey being Justice Emerson?"

The attractive and unusual high-level government couple was noticed regularly at social events and always was covered by the press. "Yesterday, at a July 4th event at the Capitol, two-fifths of the majority of the Supreme Court opinion in the latest voting rights case were seen holding hands in a quiet corner in a romantic restaurant," another reporter told his audience. The Supreme Court had never been viewed before through such a human lens.

Sydney and Jacob became a part of American judicial history. Only once before had that been a possibility—between Chief Justice William Rehnquist and Justice Sandra Day O'Connor, appointed to the Court Rehnquist later headed. When he had proposed to her after law school, he was rejected. The question never before had been raised. Sydney and Jake had a soft landing when their appointments were confirmed. They became a popular cultural story.

# chapter 12

# The Beginning of the Perfect Gender Storm

Everyone should have known it would happen. Sydney and Jake were well-known in government, by court watchers and by national organizations. She was the women's rights champion, and he was the law and order, middle-of-the-roader. When the Abdul case hit the media, everyone followed it—the public and the special interest groups, the law professors—and all of them had strong feelings about where justice lay in that case.

The basic facts were not contested; it was the perspective everyone brought to the subject which touched controversial aspects of higher education, college, and professional sports, and men and women in an era of sexual relations which was in the process of changing.

🏛

Richie Abdul was an African American high school athlete in Woodbridge, N.J. He was personable and well-liked by his class-mates and teammates. He was an OK student, mostly Bs, some Cs, one A+ (physical education). In high school he was voted "most popular" and "best athlete." Handsome and light skinned, he looked and ran like O.J. Simpson, one sports writer wrote, "but he was a sweet likable kid; not a criminal." He played football, basketball, and baseball, and he wasn't sure which he'd choose if he made it as a professional athlete. His parents hoped Princeton would lead to a professional world, beside sports. His family wanted him to have the best education and to meet a broader community than he did at his high school, which was integrated, but not too much. Princeton won the recruiting war for Richie over 60 other interested colleges.

Soon after Richie arrived at Princeton, he met Mary Marks at an entering freshman mixer. He'd been at football practice earlier and arrived late with his fellow freshman teammates on the squad. Mary was a Californian, tall, pretty, animated, a bit of a naughty mouth, smart, pre-med to follow her orthopedist father when she graduated and planned to go to medical school at UCLA or USC. She was socially forward, but in a ladylike style, and approached the attractive Richie and started a friendly conversation. They chatted animatedly most of that evening and left together. Soon they were a highly visible, mixed-race couple, a striking pair on campus, each involved in various extra-curricular activities.

Richie remained at Princeton the summer after his first year, working part-time at university jobs on campus as scholarship athletes did, and practicing with the varsity squad readying for his sophomore year. Mary returned home to California, and spent the summer and part of her second year in a semester abroad program Princeton sponsored in Paris. She returned to Princeton second semester, and she and Richie soon picked up and continued as steady social "friends." Mary worked at The Daily Princetonian newspaper (The Prince, it was called) as a columnist writing about extracurricular life on campus and as a result became well-known to her fellow students. The editor named her column "The Princeton Scene"—Mary winced—but her columns about campus activities were popular.

At the conclusion of their second year, Richie again remained on campus, and Mary returned to California where she took courses on ethics and leadership at UCLA, her focus on developing a resumé of activities to match her solid pre-med scholastic records. They corresponded, occasionally dated others casually when away from Princeton, but they continued their exclusive personal connection in their junior year. At the end of that year, shortly before their third and final summer break, what would become known later as "the Abdul case" occurred.

Later versions of the "affair" differed, as often was the case in comparable situations, but more so because both Mary and Richie were by then well-known campus celebrities and were widely seen at the school as a serious couple. She was to enter senior year as an editor of the Princetonian; Richie had become a college star, All-American by the end of his junior year, and was mentioned in sports magazines as a potential recruit for the NFL. The final week, after exams and before students left for their summer plans, Richie and Mary had a farewell date that would lead to the notorious "Abdul affair."

They had planned a pre-going-away evening beginning with dinner alone at Romeo's Ristorante, their favorite, a simple, modestly priced Italian restaurant near campus they frequented regularly. What began as a romantic goodbye evening became an edgy, charged conversation that Richie started, unintendedly.

When their drinks arrived and they had ordered, Richie

began: "You know, babe, we are from very different worlds and next year we will be heading into more separate worlds—in every sense. If we are to go ahead in our lives together, we need to deal with some touchy questions."

"What might *they* be?" she answered, put off by where the conversation seemed to be headed.

"When we graduate, where do we go next? Do we go together? Separately? We've not really dated others these past three years. Should we try dating this summer, so we know what we want to do when we return for our senior year?"

They agreed that they both would date others that summer, but the mood of their romantic evening changed, especially for Mary.

As they were finishing dinner, and stumbling around Richie's sudden awkward questions, Romeo came to the table. The place was emptying and he knew the semester was over and that these popular, regular guests would be gone for the summer. He greeted them and noticed their finished bottle of Barolo. Tired from his day's efforts, Romeo pulled over a chair and sat down with them.

"*Brindiamo insieme,*" he said to them. "Let's toast." He called over his shoulder to Luigi who was cleaning up, "*Porta un' altra bottiglia.*" Announcing to Richie and Mary, "Have another fare-well bottle with me."

They did, as their parting dinner ended, personally troubling to Mary but cheery and casual between Romeo and Richie.

Both of them were members of the elite Ivy club on campus, and they had agreed to stop by for farewells with their clubmates. Everyone had finished exams and were on their way home, so the club was packed, noisy, and boozy. Mary and Richie had some tequila shots—neither remembered how many—and by midnight they left, while the partying continued. At this point, later descriptions of what occurred varied.

Richie walked an unsteady and silent Mary back to her room, entered after her, and embraced her. No one will ever know exactly what happened next. Mary recalled nothing. Richie remembered that he didn't want their evening to end unhappily. He realized Mary was annoyed by his proposal earlier that evening over dinner, and remembered the conclusion of the evening as love-making (not unusual for them), but admittedly rough when the line between anger and desire blurred, as it sometimes does. Before he left for practice early the next morning, he kissed his sleeping lover and left a note on her desk. "I will miss you. See you in September." He sure did, but not how he imagined at the time.

Mary later admitted that she'd had too much to drink, and that Richie and she "apparently" had sex. She hadn't meant to, though in her alcoholic state she couldn't recall the details. When she awoke, Richie wasn't there. She was disheveled, still in her clothes, but her underclothes were off and strewn nearby. She felt sore and hungover. She finished packing, left hastily, and returned home later that day without seeing or hearing from Richie.

🏛

Keisha Douglas was a pal of Richie's since they arrived at Princeton, and a classmate in several courses they both took. She knew Mary, who had interviewed her once for her column about The Black Student Caucus which Keisha was a part of. Keisha and Richie were friends, buddies who'd studied together for some of their exams, but were not romantic in their closeness. All three were busy with their classes and extra-curricular activities. That third summer break, Richie and Keisha (who also worked at a university job as part of her scholarship) met at the summer students dining hall, sitting together as they often did as pals. When the subject turned to an old Spike Lee movie that was playing at the only campus film society club, they decided to go. After, Richie walked Keisha home to her room, and they both hugged and laughed about their night together. But each of them looked at the other in a way they hadn't before. They stepped away from each other momentarily, and both wondered about that "difference" after going their separate ways. They saw each other many times that summer, but always continued in a tentative, brother-sister kind of friendly relationship.

Mary returned to LA, privately angry about the last evening with Richie, at least what she could remember about it. Her family met her at the airport and en route home talked about all their summer plans. Dr. Marks had arranged an internship at Cedars, LA, a prestigious hospital where she would be working with one of his professional friends there, the impressive neurologist Dr. Sumner Samuels. That night at dinner, an old family friend and Mary's godmother, Jane Albright, a feminist litigator, joined them. After a celebratory private dinner marked by frivolous conversations between old friends catching up, Mary felt quite at home—very much in another place than Princeton. Jane had invited Mary to have lunch with her that first week of her internship, to have a "girls' chat."

They did meet later the next week at a trendy, look-over-your-shoulder-to-see-who-is-there place in Santa Monica. Jane told Mary about a sexual assault case—her specialty—that she was handling. Mary took it all in, but couldn't detach what Jane was saying about drinking and sex in one of her cases from her recent nightmarish farewell with Richie in Princeton. She didn't say anything about it to Jane, but it started her thinking about that night she couldn't remember, or forget.

A few weeks later, she decided to call Richie and explore what had happened and the meaning of that strange evening. With time differences and independent work demands, they missed each other's initial calls. At last, Richie caught her one night, late for him and just after dinner for her. After perfunctory questioning about their summers, Mary asked Richie if he was dating. "Not really, but I shared a few evenings with Keisha Douglas, remember her?"

"Yes. I know Keisha," Mary coolly responded.

Richie felt the cold breath of her voice and responded lightly, "Yeah." He and Keisha had just returned from a gospel chorus presentation on campus. "How about you?" he asked.

"I haven't had the time. And frankly, I'm upset about our farewell evening, after we left Romeo's and the Ivy party. We haven't talked since then, but we should. Perhaps when I get back in September."

"Sure," Richie replied. "Let's stay in touch meantime. I have some interesting news about professional teams interested in my future. Long story, so I'll save it. But I might be living in Green Bay, Wisconsin."

No comment from Mary. Richie sensed their distance growing, adding, "Maybe San Diego. You never know."

They never got to what was on Mary's mind. But they would. Mary called her friend Jane weeks later and asked if she might talk to her, "confidentially," about something on her mind. "Sure, honey, of course I'm your and your family's friend, but this lunch will be totally confidential. Relax." They made a date to meet later that week, this time at a quieter, more private setting, Counselor's Table, that Jane and other LA lawyers frequented— hence its name change from its original LA Chop House. They arrived separately, were quickly seated, and ordered. "Try their fish and chips, and the coleslaw is special," Jane suggested. Mary nodded. The waiter left. Jane waited for Mary to get at what was on her mind. Eventually, Mary got there.

"Jane, something has been bothering me since I returned from Princeton last month. I'm embarrassed, but after listening to you talk about one of your cases when we had lunch recently in Santa Monica, I needed to talk to someone I could trust. You'll understand why I don't wish my family involved."

"I gathered that might be the case. So before you say another word, this conversation is strictly attorney-client. I may even stick you with the bill this one and last time," she joked.

"Thanks, Jane. I need to talk about something that happened my last night in Princeton before I came home this summer." Mary then told Jane the story of her experience that last evening in Princeton, including what she remembered, and what she couldn't recall. Her story took half an hour to relate. Fish and chips came and were consumed. They lingered long after coffee and Mary told Jane her experience. The background and that last evening, all of it. Including her reaction to Richie apparently dating an African American girl, maybe moving to some godforsaken tundra city. They were, all of a sudden, and as never before, a couple from very different worlds.

After three years of colorblind love and steady dating, apparently *he* was concerned about the difference between their races! "After my life of luxury and his crawling out of his family's limited social world, now I'm facing years of poverty in medical school and internships, and Richie is about to be a multi-millionaire. I've always been—but not about to be—an enriched big city girl, and he's about to be a rich boondocks cultural hero." It seemed that after three years of public appearances as *the* couple on campus, now facing life after college, Richie was giving her a reverse "Dear John" kiss-off.

Jane was quiet a while after Mary finished. After a minute, Jane said, "Honey, yours is a story I have heard before. I know it's painful to talk about, and after our talk today and you listen to what I am going to say, then we should meet again and you can decide what option you prefer."

Jane then went on.

"Mary, honey, in the past decades, the social culture has changed. As you know, I've been in the middle of many cases with facts like yours. They are painful. Nobody really 'wins.' But important points have to be made. In your case, and others like it, it all comes down to who to believe—him or her—about consensual sex. The law now, but not always, is that consent is not consent if one party—usually the woman—is drunk and the other party—usually the man—knows it but continues to dominate the out-of-conscious woman, even if they are not strangers. In one case I handled, they were engaged to marry."

Mary was silent, listening, thinking, while Jane continued.

"You technically have a case of rape. But, as in all these cases, it will be painful if you go public with your story. Richie didn't make you drink. But he did take advantage of your being drunk. Your consent was assumed, but never given. Times have changed. Years ago, women in rape cases had their lives ruined by investigators, defense lawyers, skeptical juries. In your case, Richie is a celebrated, popular young man, about to be a millionaire."

"Yes," Mary added, "while I earn zilch for about eight years in med school and internships. How much can I ask my daddy to underwrite?"

"Money isn't, or shouldn't be, the question. Principle is the issue. And you won't be a weakling if you decided to just move on with your life. Public trials like yours are costly, emotionally and financially, and might go on a long time. You will be criticized by skeptics, like Christine Blasey Ford was when she testified to the Senate years ago about her early experience with Supreme Court Justice Kavanaugh. Why did she—why did you—wait for months to complain? Don't underestimate what will happen to you if you go forward with your complaint. Will it be worth it?"

Mary pondered her question. She was growing up. How would she like to be described later, in her obituary? Controversial feminist whistleblower, or the celebrated first female surgeon to perform a heart transplant?

That decision wouldn't be made over lunch. But it preoccupied Mary's thoughts in the ensuing months while she was in California.

A week before she was to return to Princeton, Mary called Jane.

"Can we have another lunch, counselor? I think I know what I have to do. But I need you to walk me through all the steps."

🏛

Love and hate, devotion and disgruntlement, can be so close, it can surprise people when they encounter the change. As Mary brooded after her talk with her godmother, she felt humiliated. Yes, she and Richie did face important questions about their future when he questioned her about it in that last conversation at Romeo's. And yes, she didn't have an answer about their future when he raised the question. But cynicism and sexploitation grew in her mind as she pondered whether his recent "friendship" with Keisha was the real motive for his questions to her. And the specifics of her clouded recollection of their sex in her room took on a darker perspective. He'd always used protection when they had sex, and there was no sign of a used condom in her room. Might his behavior have been digital? In any event, she was sore in body and in mind, thinking about his kiss-off note. She hadn't gone to the university infirmary the following morning to be sure she wasn't pregnant, or injured?

Every part of what she had thought about Richie now took on a new and negative connotation. No longer the sweet, likeable student athlete, nor the fine, proud All-American; he now was the typical rich and famous jock, fulfilled by his screwing Ms. Whitey. She realized she had to do something about it. She was sure it would become a parochial Princeton gender contretemps that would generate side-taking, female vs. male. But how could she *not* expose Richie? How would she explain her and Richie's breakup, and all its cultural undertones? Who had left whom?

Princeton had a procedure, she learned. She could file a complaint to the provost office, which would assign a neutral hearing officer to consider all complaints seriously, confidentially, and do the right and proper thing. Her delay in doing so would be seen as a product of the end of the semester. She wouldn't let her grievance continue to fester. The very day she returned, she went to the proper administrative office and filed her succinct confidential complaint. Her first column that week at The Daily Princetonian was titled "Will This Ever Change?" Without disclosing her personal experience or complaint, she wrote a strong editorial on the subject of the predatory problem of dating on campus—the continuing global problem, not her personal complaint, readers assumed. At first.

She didn't share her own complaint to friends who mentioned the article, or to readers who commented to her about it. Everyone complimented her probing opinion piece. She didn't see Richie those first few days—everyone was busy doing their thing. But when he called to see how and where she was, she replied coldly, "Getting on with my life," and hung up. It would be many days before he saw her and learned what was happening.

# chapter 13

# The Wheels of Justice

The treatment of sexual crimes historically prejudiced women accusers who had traumatic experiences that were compounded when they were made public. Some countries and cultures shamed them and their families, even committed further violences against them. Until the 21st century, this uphill battle women faced when they reported being raped led many of them to fear making public complaints, and instead to endure their hurt and shame privately. That approach began to change as a result of women's movements for justice in the late 20th century and early 21st century.

In the 1990s, the Supreme Court ruled that under Title VII of the Civil Rights Act, the Department of Education should deny federal money if a recipient college had "actual knowledge" of sexual misconduct on campus and responded with "deliberate indifference." Only if the conduct was "so severe, persistent, and objectively offensive that it effectively bars the victim's access to educational opportunity," would complaints be processed. That "head in the sand" approach led the Supreme Court in 2001 to require more protective standards. But for a decade its mandate was neglected.

When the Obama administration discovered that one in five women were being sexually assaulted in college due to the prevailing campus culture, it promulgated new regulations.

They defined sexual harassment as "any unwelcome conduct of a sexual nature." They required schools to use a more lenient "preponderance of the evidence" standard ("50% plus a feather"), and discouraged contentious live hearings and hostile trial-like cross-examination. One appointed investigator was to determine guilt or innocence, acting in effect as prosecutor, judge, and jury.

In the Trump era, Secretary of Education Betsy DeVos sought to move things back to the earlier, pre-Obama era, focusing less on harassment than serious sexual misconduct. Live hearings were required, and the accused was required to have the right to cross-examine complainants. The Department's civil rights chief interpreted the Department's policy to "faithfully execute the laws as written and in full, no more and no less."

Those became the prevailing rules in the appeal of *Abdul v. Princeton University*. Ray Brown, Richie's retained counsel in the legal dispute and a well-known local civil rights trial lawyer, focused on the new due process requirements, that courts must require alleged perpetrators to be able to appear and personally cross-examine complainants. He emphasized that the more rigorous, clear and convincing standard of evidence should now be applied, and that the accused must have the right to appeal the school's decision. Were universities biased to favor women in order to protect their financial interests in receiving government funding?

Jane Albright argued—as did supportive women's groups— that such an adversarial procedure would re-traumatize young victims, discourage complaints, and make the process unnecessarily trial-like.

That was the history the Supreme Court later had to deal with in the Abdul case when it later got there. The parties' two attorneys were sophisticated, experienced lawyers, and as evidence of the conundrum of the case, both relied in their trial and appellate briefs on the same 2020 Brookings Institution analysis to make their points. Richie's lawyer pointed out that the complainant had a lawyer; his client did not. He did not even know about the complaint, nor was he allowed to appear to defend himself. The hearing officer was judge and jury. "How can those facts constitute due process of law?"

Jane Albright argued, citing the same Brookings analysis, that Richie now did have estimable counsel, and that campus regulations have been and need to remain less rigorous than courtroom trials, or students dating would have to video their love lives, and the life on college campuses would be so potentially adversarial that students would need to have attorneys as roommates.

Under the Obama administration regulations—referred to as the Clery Act—prior rules governing sexual and dating assaults on campus had been expanded to the benefit of young women. Based on recommendations of an advisory panel of prior student victims, advocacy groups, law enforcement representatives, and colleges, the new rules added categories of victims (men as well as women), a more inclusive definition of rape, and confidential procedures to assure prompt, fair, and impartial on-campus private hearings. Reformers and women's groups had managed to tilt the balance back in favor of women who had been ignored and prejudiced in the past, critics of the new law complained.

Most feminist groups that Sydney had historically supported in articles and important court decisions later were
outraged that President Trump and his Education Secretary
would take women's rights a giant step back to the attitudes of
earlier eras, again ignoring the traditional prejudices faced by
aggrieved women. Men's advocacy organizations supported the
new change. Public comments about the regulation were a "tsu-
nami," the press reported. About 125,000 comments supported
the proposed change.

It was a classic example of one right violating another right.
And who would be hurt more by the Court's eventual ruling?

▥

This was the situation at the start of her senior year when Mary
presented her complaint to the university provost, who quickly
appointed Karen Forché, a female professor from the School
of Graduate Affairs, to be her hearing officer. None of this
was made public. At her hearing, Mary presented an affidavit from Jane Albright attesting to Mary's seeking her confidential advice the prior summer as an attorney, offered partly
to preclude any question about why she waited all summer to
make her complaint, and partially to make it clear she had been
advised and would be represented by a well-known women's
rights lawyer. Richie never knew about any of this, and since
Mary's complaint was dated and she was OK and back at school,
Richie wasn't called by the hearing officer.

Within a month, after consulting confidentially with a constitutional law professor on the Princeton faculty and with the

president of the university at the time (this would be a contentious case considering the parties, one of whom was now a public figure), the university's initial decision on Mary's complaint was confirmed by Forché based on the former prevailing wording of the relevant law about the subject and the mores of that time. A formal letter on university stationery was personally delivered to Richie. A copy was sent to Mary and her counsel, Jane Albright.

When Richie opened the letter, thinking it might be an entreaty from another NFL team, not the first, he was "what-the-hell" stunned. He took it to his fatherly, mentoring coach who also was puzzled and shocked. The coach had known Mary as Richie's girlfriend for years and advised him to see the author of the letter, no less than Daniel Fromer, the highly respected president of Princeton. The president would not see Richie alone and recommended he seek a counsel of his own if he intended to appeal this matter. Suddenly, this was the darkest hour of Richie's previously charmed life.

Richie told only his family, who were abashed and feared their star son's life would be ruined when his newsworthy dismissal "without prejudice" went public (as if that fact could not be *per se* prejudicial). He was referred by supporters to Ray Brown, a successful African American trial lawyer in Jersey City who would appeal Richie's case. They couldn't do more with the university, Ray advised, but they could and would appeal to the federal trial court in Newark, arguing that Richie was prejudiced by an unconventional hearing where he had been denied "the fundamental right under the US Constitution to confront and cross-examine his accuser, and present his defense, a brutal example of the denial of due process," in Ray Brown's words. As the case he filed in Newark was a public record, the complaint attached the letter from Princeton's president, and Richie's protest letter of denial (prepared by Ray Brown). An expeditious hearing was requested, along with an injunction against dismissal until Richie was given "a fair hearing, which would be his first," the complaint emphasized. The court granted a temporary injunction and ordered an expedited hearing on the merits of his dismissal. Richie continued his final year at Princeton, but under a cloud.

The national press jumped on the salacious story, with front pages, sports pages, opinion columns by pundits opining from all perspectives. The judicious Princeton University student paper offered the student body balanced but continuing coverage, making it clear that Mary would not be writing about the case, and that she and Richie would be given the opportunity to comment should they wish to. Neither did, on advice of counsel. But for both, their final months at Princeton were "different." Mary focused on completing her pre-med curriculum. Richie was pursued by several professional teams, but not nearly as many as he thought would be the case before "the Mary affair."

The hearing on the merits of *Abdul v. Princeton University* went forward expeditiously by federal court practice standards; but it was not until the parties' second semester that Ray Brown and Jane Albright would meet in court on the merits of the then celebrated case. The courtroom was packed, as was the press box. Jane called Mary as her first witness and she related her version of their final "date," as Jane sarcastically referred to the event in question. Mary was dressed conservatively, spoke slow and haltingly, clearly distressed if composed. Jane also called an expert witness, a renowned public advocate for women's rights at that time, who was a good witness, well-known and credentialled. Between the testimony of Mary and her expert, Professor Forché, the hearing officer mechanically replayed a tape of their hearing, and described her advice from Princeton community experts, despite Ray's objection that it was "damaging, and improper hearsay."

Richie was Ray's first witness. He was personable, seemed older and more adult than Mary, and made a good case explaining why he himself was a victim in the ongoing battle of the sexes, and at a particularly prejudicial, reputational time in his future life work striving to be a role model as a professional athlete. There were more women than men on the jury, and as many black as white. Ray Brown eloquently told the jurors that this case involved a clear right versus a questionable wrong. He was solicitous of Mary but ardently presented Richie's side of the event, "for the first time," he kept repeating, carefully and respectfully urging that a dispassionate jury would have to determine a challenging decision between two credible and attractive young people. One of them, Ray pointed out, had already been prejudiced and stigmatized in his blooming career, after never having had the opportunity to tell his side of the event to the few Princeton officials who simply decided to throw him out of school. All this, in his final year, without evidence of his wrongdoing "beyond a reasonable doubt," as the judge would instruct them was the proper standard to guide them in its deliberations.

The jury came back in less than two hours with a verdict, granting Richie's injunction request and ordering Princeton to graduate him so he would not be prejudiced by its prior improper action against Richie. Ray and Richie hugged; then his parents hugged them both, and Ray took all four to a celebratory lunch. The national press and The Princetonian covered the trial extensively. Jane told reporters that she would appeal this verdict to the federal Court of Appeals. Mary was instructed to defer all questions to Jane while the appeal went forward. Ray spoke to the press on the steps of the courthouse, stating sarcastically he never had a doubt that the Princeton officials had "lynched" Richie without even hearing his side of the story, as the jury did. "What way is this for a university to act? What kind of lesson does Princeton provide by such preemptory behavior? Their officials need to take a course on constitutional law," Ray sarcastically remarked. "Perhaps at Rutgers, my alma mater," he teased as a reverse spin on "elite" and expensive schools.

Richie was seriously courted by four teams and eventually chosen by the Green Bay Packers, who invited him to rookie camp after choosing him as the fourth pick in that year's draft. Richie liked the idea of playing for a legendary team, far from Princeton and New Jersey for the first time in his life. He was a rich, happy, successful man.

The Court of Appeals panel of three reversed the trial court decision (2–1), and then Ray Brown appealed to the full federal court of appeals (eleven members, including the original three members who voted to reverse the trial court's ruling protecting Richie's college career). Ray Brown and Jane Albright would meet again in the august courtroom in Philadelphia, to plead the appeal of their colleagues' 2–1 vote in favor of Mary's position. By then, Mary was in medical school at UCLA, and Richie was playing his first season as a running back for the Green

Bay Packers. The full federal appeals court voted 6–5 to uphold Princeton's dismissal of Richie. As a matter of law, the university had followed its own rules implementing the prevailing federal law in this case, and if that federal law was to be changed, the change should have come from Congress, the court deferentially ruled.

Ray Brown petitioned for *certiorari*, asking the Supreme Court to review the two preceding split votes by the circuit court. "Critical issues of due process law initially were settled by a jury on fundamental questions in favor of Mr. Abdul, as it should have, and the constitutional law demands it should be in this case," he pleaded. He cited a recent case holding that "what is fundamentally fair is always a context-specific inquiry," and Princeton never allowed his client to tell his side of the story. As is the custom, petitions for *certiorari* require four votes for the court to take a case, and for the third time in the Abdul case, the Supreme Court (four of its members) decided that the case should come forward.

By the time the court records reached the Supreme Court, 17 states and many amicus briefs by women's groups had joined in asking the Department of Education and the courts to prevent the new rule from taking effect.

Mary was in residency in her third year of medical school, and Richie was in Green Bay, his agent negotiating a new ten-year contract that would place Richie in an elite circle in professional sports.

*chapter 14*

# Evening the Scales of Justice

Periodically, the justices met privately in their oak-paneled conference room in the Chief Justice's chambers. It was spare and sound-proof, with marble fireplaces and glass chandeliers sheltered by double doors. Bookcases of the Court's opinions lined the walls. The justices wore no robes and followed their venerable routine that began with multiple formal but cordial handshakes. They sat around a rectangular table in black leather chairs, bearing on their backs each justice's nameplate.

In the custom of these private weekly meetings of the justices, not accompanied by staff or other assistants, the Chief Justice would go around the table in reverse order of longevity, from the newest justice to the longest-sitting colleague, and ask for comments about each case where *certiorari* had been granted. Then, assessing where the majority of votes was likely—that could change—he would assign one justice to write a draft of the majority opinion, and another the dissent.

In *Abdul v. Princeton University*, one justice recused herself because she was a Princeton graduate with close ties to her alma mater. That left eight justices, hopefully not split 4–4 on this celebrated case on such a hot topic. A 4–4 decision would leave the lower appellate court's 6–5 ruling against Richie as the prevailing one. The Chief Justice assigned Jake, the newest member of the court, to try his hand at the likely majority (it would take five votes of the eight, at least). If his draft opinion did not get four or five votes, the Chief Justice would then assign the majority opinion to one of the minority members who did not agree with Jake's proposed majority opinion. "This will help you earn your spurs, Jacob," the Chief Justice Jones stated, to the smiles of the other judges who all looked toward Sydney.

Jake and Sydney usually discussed the cases before the Court, but they didn't about the Abdul case. Jake presumed Sydney would be for affirming the last Court of Appeals decision, upholding Princeton's right to follow the prevailing federal law when it had its hearing years before.

Sydney and Jake had decided not to discuss privately their tentative, presumed inclinations to be on opposite sides of the two four-member positions. Ray Brown argued to the Court that federal laws which governed years ago had been changed by Congress and that current legislation should be followed now by the Court—especially when highly charged constitutional issues were involved. Jane argued on Mary's behalf that the prevailing rule at the time should govern the propriety of the proceeding then.

Jake went ahead drafting an opinion based on the Constitution's due process of law clause which he thought would be balanced enough to pick up the few unpredictable votes that might make a five-vote majority. When his first draft was circulated, only three other justices signed on, and Sydney wasn't one of them. Nor had she signed onto another proposed dissenting opinion. Jake tried to modify his draft plea for the supremacy of constitutional rights in cases where important rights clash.

When his clerk gathered the second round of votes, there were three dissenters to Jake's proposed opinion, not four. Sydney had written a separate concurring opinion that added to Jacob's four votes, which then became a governing five.

Jake wrote a clear, dispassionate opinion about the sources of and reasons for the Sixth Amendment requirements. The right for counsel to defend oneself is fundamental to all of a defendant's rights, and integral to the confrontation and cross-examination and fair trial clauses, he wrote, because without counsel *all* defense rights are meaningless.

Jake did include in his scholarly analysis one reference to the late Supreme Court Justice Ruth Bader Ginsburg, a known and respected feminist, on the appropriate balance between due process and protecting gender equality: "The person who is accused has a right to defend herself or himself, and we certainly should not lose sight of that . . . complaints should be heard . . . 'college codes of conduct,' Ginsberg stated, must assure 'the accused person a fair opportunity to be heard, and that is one of the basic tenets of our system . . . everyone deserves a fair hearing." On balancing the value of due process against the need for gender equality, Justice Ginsburg had stated, 'It's not one or the other. It's both . . . people who are accused get due process.' When Justice Ginsburg died, equal rights groups published a note on her passing, repeating her lifelong message: 'Equal Means Equal.'"

Jake understood that his opinion was based on the Sixth Amendment's history, and he wrote a scholarly draft opinion which traced the history and evolution of the rights to counsel, confrontation, and cross-examination from English common law to colonial law to modern law. As lawyers were given greater powers at trials, defendants' rights expanded. But it took a very long time. Jake's extensive and well-documented opinion would become an authority on constitutional law more so than the facts of *Abdul v. Princeton*. He quoted key cases on these points: "The trial system had been transformed when defense counsel became able to cross-examine witnesses, not solely to determine sentences," he pointed out. The hearsay rule required these procedural rights, so evidence in the search for truth would have limits. He quoted words of Chief Justice John Marshall in the Aaron Burr case in 1807, and literature from the notorious Salem Witch Trials. The whole trial process was changed when lawyers' roles were expanded, and American law has protected and expanded these Sixth Amendment rights increasingly to the present time. These Bill of Rights Amendments go to the heart of the adversary process and the need for checks and balances, he underscored.

Jake's opinion was wide-ranging and academic, summarizing the law from England in earlier centuries, colonial law, and modern law to the present. It avoided the more political, often contentious underlying arguments about gender rights, as it had to if he was to gather a majority of five. Due process guides courts, he added, and it must guide universities when they are acting in a quasi-judicial capacity.

Sydney's concurring opinion commented briefly about the now majority opinion, referring to it as "an exhaustive and authoritative history of the Sixth Amendment, with which I concur. To the point that the majority avoided, understandably, I add further comments," she continued.

"I reach my conclusion to join the majority, cognizant that

some observers may view the Court's decision as a departure from well-known and widely accepted public views on the need to modernize women's rights. But, history demonstrates that being a feminist fundamentally means demanding equality, not the blind and automatic following of a party line on all issues. All orthodoxies are dangerous and to be avoided in favor of reason and precedent. Generalities may be correct; but so also may be exceptions to them. Therefore, I concur with the majority's determination that due process of law is important—and underscore that it should be available to men and women, equally. To even the playing field, as some have demanded, correctly, the field must be evened. *All* students must be treated fairly. If petitioner Abdul had been a woman, surely the most ardent feminists would applaud the conclusion on equality of constitutional rights reached here on behalf of the appellant, Mr. Abdul, by the majority."

After the decision was made public, reporters ran to the halls and outside steps with their cell phones to report their stories. "Breaking News!" the TV media led with the Supreme Court ruling. Later that day, Sydney received a call in her chambers from Kevin McCarthy at the Washington Post. She knew Kevin from her earlier days in Washington as the hot young reporter Jake had dealings with. Now, Kevin was the elder statesman at the Post, and he was curious about whether there was any "back story" of her and Jake's opinion in the now celebrated Abdul case.

"Any pillow talk?" he teased.

"Yes," Sydney teased back, "I refused to recuse myself!"

That evening, as Sydney and Jake walked from the Court to their nearby condo, they spoke of the case informally for the first time.

"That was a strong but chancy concurring opinion you wrote," Jake remarked to Sydney as they strolled home. "Did you hear from your friends on the Committee?"

"One discrete call from Val. She said I was right, your opinion was balanced."

"What did you say to her about upholding the position of President Trump and Secretary DeVos?"

"Even a blind pig occasionally will find a truffle," Sydney answered.

"That remark should go in your unauthorized bio."

"Did I surprise you?" she answered.

"You sure did, and our colleagues will never believe we didn't settle this one under the covers," Jake smiled, squeezing Sydney's hand.

Sydney answered, "Well, never too late for that. As Humphrey Bogart said to Claude Rains walking away from the foggy airport in Casablanca, 'This could be the beginning of a beautiful friendship.'"

"And, three more votes and we'll have a majority into the future."

Mary changed from her planned specialty in med school to psychiatry, a subject that absorbed her as a student and led to postgraduate studies in the field. She would privately ponder through later years what had truly happened with her and Richie that night in question. She eventually married an emergency room doctor she had met at med school and they settled in LA.

Richie's days in Green Bay earned him a fortune. He injured his knee seriously in the fifth year of his ten-year extension, and after a year of avid but frustrated rehab, he decided reluctantly that it was time to move on with his life. He was such a popular personality that an announcing job kept him close to the game that had changed his and his family's lives. He had a public social career, often paired with notable film actresses and media figures, and ended up marrying the sports doctor who had nurtured his rehab treatment.

*chapter 15*

# Pause

Sydney and Jake (Justices Emerson and Lehman) remained on the Supreme Court for twenty years. The Abdul case was not the last of their remarkable opinions for the Supreme Court. Nor were their second lives in the nation's capital the last of their life surprises. Those too could fill a book.

# ACKNOWLEDGEMENTS

My thanks to Gerrie Sturman and Steven Seigart, who assisted me in the beginning and concluding of my work, and to Stephanie Beard and her colleagues Heather Howell, Ezra Fitz, Kathleen Timberlake, and Lauren Ash, who improved it.